THE SIREN'S LAMENT

JUN'ICHIRŌ TANIZAKI

THE SIREN'S LAMENT

Essential Stories

Translated from the Japanese by
Bryan Karetnyk

PUSHKIN PRESS
LONDON

Pushkin Press
Somerset House, Strand
London WC2R 1LA

English translation © Bryan Karetnyk 2023

First published by Pushkin Press in 2023

1 3 5 7 9 8 6 4 2

ISBN 13: 978-1-78227-809-2

Frontispiece: © GL Archive / Alamy Stock Photo

Designed and typeset by Tetragon, London
Printed and bound in Great Britain by TJ Books, Padstow, Cornwall

www.pushkinpress.com

Contents

PREFACE

Jun'ichirō Tanizaki (1886–1965) was a titan of Japanese letters. His formidable career, which had an immeasurable influence on the development of modern Japanese literature, spanned more than half a century and three imperial eras, as well as Japan's rise and precipitous fall as a colonial power. Yet while, throughout those tumultuous years, the bundan, Japan's literary establishment, was often predominated by so much conventionalism and orthodoxy—first by the bleakly confessional brand of naturalism known as the 'I-novel', and latterly by a vogue for Marxism and socially informed 'proletarian' writing—Tanizaki's fiction cut conspicuously, defiantly, perversely against the grain.

Rejecting both the mundane prosaicism of the I-novel and the stringently grim, propagandistic code of proletarian fiction, Tanizaki's often alarming and disturbing fantasies sooner aimed at something at once more universal and essential: the splendour and horror of man's desires, paramount among which was an unremitting obsession with love, lust, and longing. Founded on an unshakeable belief in art's prerogative to transcend the quotidian, Tanizaki's is an *œuvre* that delights in portraying, with opulent detail and ruthless penetration, fictional worlds that explore the pathos and violence of humanity's darker urges, the sado-masochistic yearning to dominate and be dominated, the destructive power of eros and decadence, and the paper-thin line between the sublime and the depraved.

The three stories included in this short collection are taken from the audacious early years of Tanizaki's career and celebrate the precocious genius of a young author already at the forefront of international literary modernism and on the cusp of artistic maturity. The first piece, 'The Qilin' (*Kirin*), which was first published in the review *Shinshichō* in 1910, ventures away from Japan—overseas and into the mists of antiquity and legend. Steeped in classical references to the history and philosophy of ancient China, Tanizaki's narrative places the extremities of desire and caprice in the hands of the powerful, reimagining an episode of Confucius' travels in the state of Wei, where an oppressed people hopes that the Great Sage may teach its rulers 'a lesson in grace and wise government'. Finding the sovereign there in thrall to an evil and luxurious woman, Confucius discovers that he must vie for the mind of the

virtuous but biddable duke with an individual whose magnificence is matched only by her iniquity. At her command,
scenes of extraordinary beauty and sensuality are conjured
up, taking on grotesque proportions and culminating in
a sadistic *ne plus ultra*: a garden scene, in which the reader
anticipates an earthly paradise filled with exotic rarities,
only to find a haunting hellscape fit to rival any nightmare
of Hieronymus Bosch. In place of a would-be arcadia, we
are made witness to a gruesome vista of the oppressed and
terrorized populace, 'a crowd of the damned in the midst
of cruel tortures', all wantonly maimed and disfigured,
'soaked in crimson, like peonies in full bloom'—the very
sight of which plunges the diabolical consort into a state
of ecstasy and rapture. Even virtue, warns Tanizaki, may
be corrupted by power and status and bent to such lavish
and extravagant obscenity.

'Killing O-Tsuya' (*Otsuya-koroshi*), which debuted in the
literary journal *Chūō Kōron* in 1915, returns the reader to
Japan, but to the city of Edo (now Tokyo) in the days of
the military government that was the Tokugawa shogunate.
There, in Tanizaki's native city, amid the perilous back-
streets and pleasure quarters of the 'downtown' Shitamachi
and along the moonlit waterways of the Sumida river,
we catch a violent glimpse of the culture of geisha and
courtesans, gangsters and cut-throats. As we follow the

young and naïve Shinsuke while he goes to any and all ends in pursuit of his love for his master's manipulative daughter O-Tsuya, we observe the pair's slow descent into a pit of corruption and depravity, by way of illicit love, theft, debauchery, vice, and, eventually, murder. Structured along the lines of a kabuki play and embellished with all manner of overt and subtle references to the theatre and a theatricalized world, the work presents a cat's cradle of shifting identities, allegiances, and disguises, which are staged and upended with arresting artistic bravura. Moreover, as Tanizaki pushes his characters ever closer to the brink of their own tragedies, he maintains a masterly ambiguity and dramatic tension right until the dark denouement of the final scene, which draws the work to its brutal close by the waterfront in Mukōjima.

In the final piece of this collection, 'The Siren's Lament' (*Ningyo no nageki*), which appeared in *Chūō Kōron* precisely two years after 'Killing O-Tsuya', Tanizaki transports the reader back to China, although now not to the remote antiquity of the Spring and Autumn Period, but to the decadence of the late imperial era in the eighteenth century, 'when the House of Aisin-Gioro sat upon the dragon throne and the Qing dynasty still flourished with all the dazzling splendour of peonies in June'. In this fairy tale tinged with a note of tender nostalgia, a handsome and listless prince who has exhausted every extreme of earthly dissipation yearns for new sensations to satiate his desires both subtle and gross. So it happens that, one day, while languishing in his palace, he receives a visit from an outlandish Dutch merchant, who purports to be selling a beautiful and priceless rarity: a European mermaid, which captivates him, heart and soul. In the work's ostentatious conflation of Chinese, Japanese, and European histories, Tanizaki confects a unique fable that estranges occidentalist and orientalist assumptions and blurs the borders between dream and reality. As the melancholy prince embarks upon his ill-fated final quest for happiness and fulfilment, the reader is left contemplating the sublime pleasures and psychological devastation wrought by such longing for chimeras.

These three works are, of course, essential in that they capture early expressions of the themes for which Tanizaki would later win worldwide acclaim in his major novels; more importantly, however, they are also essential in terms of their exuberant, unflinching exploration of humanity's darkest impulses and desires, from the most base to the most exquisite. 'Here is a writer,' the great Kafū Nagai wrote of Tanizaki's short fiction as early as 1911, 'who has successfully explored artistic territory that nobody else in contemporary Japanese literature has yet been able, or dared, to tackle.' Tanizaki's writing was indeed an act of daring—one that looked human imperfection in the eye and had the boldness of imagination to transfigure it into the most ravishing, unsettling art.

B.S.K.

THE QILIN

Phoenix! O phoenix!
How thy virtue hath declined.
What hath come to pass cannot be put aright,
but what is still to come may be avoided yet.
Give up thy vain pursuit. Give it up, I say.
Dangerous are those who now administer the affairs of state.

ACCORDING TO the chronicles of Zuo Qiuming and Meng Ke, of Sima Qian and others, at the beginning of spring in the year 493 before the birth of Christ, in the thirteenth year of the Duke Ding's reign in the state of Lu, when the ruler was celebrating the Festival of the Heavens and the Earth, Confucius, together with a handful of disciples attending his carriage, left the land of his birth to preach the Way abroad.

On the banks of the Sishui river, fragrant green grasses were sprouting, and although the snow was melting on the summits of Mount Fang, Mount Niqiu and Wu Peak, a northern wind that swooped down, like hordes of Huns whipping up the sands of the desert, still brought back memories of a harsh winter. Full of energy, Zilu led the group, his lilac robes with their marten trim flapping in the wind. Behind him followed Yan Yuan, his gaze pensive, and with him the zealous and devoted Zeng Shen, both of their feet clad in shoes of bast. The very embodiment of virtue, the driver Fan Chi gripped the reins of the four horses, and, between furtive glances at the wizened face of the Great Sage riding in the carriage, he would ponder the bitter lot of this wandering teacher and let fall a tear.

One day, when at last they had reached the frontier of the state of Lu, each of the men looked back wistfully towards his native land, but the road by which they had come was hidden in the shadow of the so-called 'tortoise' mountain, Mount Gui. Then Confucius, picking up his zither, sang in a mournful, hoarse voice:

> I long to see my land of Lu,
> But it is shaded by Mount Gui.
> Should I now go and bear an axe
> And hew its tortoise shell away?

They journeyed further and further to the north and, after three days, found themselves amid a vast plain where they heard a voice singing a peaceful and carefree song. It was an old man garbed in deerskin and with a rope for a belt, humming to himself as he gathered ears of grain that had fallen by the wayside.

'You, what does this song say to you?' asked Confucius, turning to Zilu.

'The old man's song has not the lofty melancholy that echoes in those of the Master. He sings freely, like a bird in the sky.'

'Quite so. This is none other than a disciple of the late Laozi. His name is Linlei and he must be a good hundred years old. But, with the arrival of spring each year, he comes out into the fields and sings as he gathers grain. Let one of you go over there and speak to him.'

No sooner had Confucius' words been spoken than Zigong, one of the disciples, rushed over to the edge of the field and greeted the old man, asking him:

'You sing your song and gather up the fallen ears of grain, old man, but have you no regrets in life?'

Without turning around, the old man just went on picking the fallen ears of grain diligently, all the while singing in time with the steps he took. Zigong followed him and called out again. The old man finally stopped singing and looked at Zigong intently.

'What should I have to regret?' said the old man.

'In your youth, you were unobservant. As you grew, you did not contest your time. And in maturity, with neither wife nor child, and though the hour of your death approaches, you take some pleasure in gathering ears of grain and singing songs.'

The old man roared with laughter.

'My pleasures are known to every man, though they turn them into sorrows. Yes, I was unobservant in my youth. Yes, I let my time go uncontested. Yes, I have neither wife nor child in my old age. And yes, the hour of my death does approach at last. This, therefore, is why I am happy.'

'But if to wish for a long life, as every man does, means to fear death, then how is it that you can rejoice in its approach?' Zigong asked again.

'Life and death are but a departure and a return. To die here is to be born there. I know that to cling to life is a futile act. To die today, to be born yesterday: I doubt there is much difference.'

Having said this, the old man carried on singing. Zigong had failed to apprehend the meaning of his words, but when he returned and relayed them to the Great Sage, Confucius said:

'The old man can certainly talk, but I can see that he has not yet fully understood the Way.'

They journeyed on for many days and more, and crossed the Jishui river. The black cloth hat worn by the Sage was covered in dust, and his fox-trimmed robes had faded in the rain and wind.

'The Sage by the name of Kong Qiu has arrived from the state of Lu. May he teach our tyrannical sovereign and his consort a lesson in grace and wise government!'

Such were the comments made in the street as the people pointed to the carriage and its procession as it entered the capital of the state of Wei. The people here had grown emaciated with hunger and toil, and the walls of their houses sighed with grief and sorrow. All the lovely flowers of this land had been transplanted to the palace to delight the eyes of the sovereign's consort, while the plump boars had been taken and served up to please her sophisticated tastes. And so, the tranquil spring sun shone in vain on the grey, deserted streets of the city. And, perched atop a hill in the centre, the palace, shining with the five colours of the rainbow, towered over the corpse of the capital like a beast of prey. The ringing of a bell from the depths of the palace thundered throughout the four corners of the city like the roar of a wild animal.

'What does the sound of that bell say to you?' Confucius again asked Zilu.

'Its sound is unlike the fleeting, spontaneous songs of the Master that call up to the heavens, nor is it like the melodies of Linlei that are freely entrusted to the cosmos. Rather, its tolling speaks of something terrible, glorifying sinful pleasures that run counter to the will of heaven.'

'Quite so. That is the so-called Grove Bell, which in former days the Duke Xiang of Wei had struck from the treasures and the sweat that he extorted from his subjects. When the bell is rung, its echo reverberates from one grove of the palace garden to the next, producing the most awe-inspiring sound. Its ringing is so dreadful because it contains the curses and tears of those tormented by the tyrant.'

Thus spoke Confucius.

The ruler of Wei, the Duke Ling, had ordered that a mica screen and a sofa inlaid with agate be placed by the parapet of the Tower of Spirits, which looked out over his royal demesne; he stood there in the company of his consort, Nanzi, who was enveloped in a cloud of blue robes with a long, iridescent train, and, while pouring for each other cups of a richly perfumed millet liqueur, they admired the spring fields and mountains slumbering beneath a thick shroud of mist.

'The beautiful light flows like a stream, flooding both heaven and earth. Yet why do we not see gaily coloured flowers in the houses of our people? Why do we not hear the cheerful singing of birds?' the Duke asked, furrowing his brow in displeasure.

'It is because the people, not content with praising the clemency of Your Serene Highness and the beauty of His Serene Highness's consort, pay homage by bringing all the beautiful plants without exception to adorn the palace gardens; every bird in the land gathers there, attracted by the scent of these flowers,' answered the eunuch Yong Qu, who was attending his lord and master.

At that moment, breaking the silence of the deserted streets, the jade bell of Confucius' carriage rang brilliantly as it passed beneath the tower.

The General, Wangsun Jia, who was also in attendance of the sovereign, widened his eyes in surprise. 'Who is the person riding in that carriage?' he asked. 'He has the brow of Yao, the eyes of Shun, the nape of Gao Yao and the shoulders of Zichan! He would have the legs of Yu, as well, were they but three *cun* longer.'

'But how sad he looks!' exclaimed Nanzi, before turning to the officer and pointing towards the speeding carriage. 'Tell me, General, you who are the fount of all knowledge: from which land does he hail?'

'In my youth I visited many lands in our realm, but, with the exception of Lao Dan, who served as chronicler at the royal court of Zhou, never have I encountered a man with such a noble mien. This can only be Confucius, the Sage who, having grown disillusioned with the government in his native Lu, has taken to the road to spread his teaching. It is said that at his birth a chimera—a *qilin*—appeared, harmonious music filled the sky, and a goddess descended from the heavens. The mouth of the Sage evokes the power of the bull, his hands the strength of the tiger, and his back the hardy shell of the tortoise. Standing at a height of nine *chi* and six *cun*, he has the bearing and stature of King Wen. It is undoubtedly he,' Wangsun Jia explained.

'This Sage of whom you speak, what art does he teach?' asked the Duke Ling as he drained his cup.

'Sages hold the key to all earthly knowledge,' the General replied. 'But that man, it seems, is interested solely in bringing to rulers the art of governance: that of ensuring order in their houses, of making their nations prosper and of pacifying their realms.'

'I searched for earthly beauties and found Nanzi. I gathered treasures from the four corners of the world and built this palace. Now I should like to rule supreme, to adorn myself with the authority befitting of such a wife and such a palace. By all means, summon this Sage here that I may learn from him the art of subjugating everything under heaven.'

With these words, the Duke peered directly across the table at his wife's lips, for ordinarily the words that issued from them expressed his true sentiments more faithfully than did his own words.

'I should like to see with my own eyes any and all of the extraordinary creatures in this world,' said Nanzi. 'If that man of mournful countenance is indeed a sage, he will no doubt be able to show me many wonders.'

With that, she lifted her dreaming eyes and followed the carriage as it raced off into the distance.

Confucius and his disciples were approaching the North Palace when a team of four horses arrived in full force. Accompanied by a large retinue, an official of wise countenance stepped out of the carriage and greeted the wanderers with all due deference.

'I am your humble servant Zhongshu Yu, sent to welcome you by order of His Serene Highness the Duke Ling. It is known now in every corner of the realm that the Master has taken to the road to spread his teaching. Over the course of your long journey, your jade-coloured canopy has become frayed by the wind, and the axle of your carriage has begun to creak. May it please you to take this new carriage and grace the palace with your presence, so that you might reveal to our sovereign the wisdom of the rulers of antiquity, who knew how to govern and bring peace to their domains. To alleviate your fatigue, the crystal waters of a bubbling hot spring await you at the southern end of the West Garden. To quench your thirst, the orchards of the palace are overflowing with fragrant yuzu, sweet pomelo, bitter orange and tangerine. To amuse your palate, you will find dozing in the cages of the royal park wild boar, bears, leopards, oxen and sheep, all nicely fattened and with bellies like eiderdown. May it please you to stay in our land for two months, three months, a year, ten years even, to dissipate the mists that cloud our minds and open our blinded eyes for to see.'

'The sincere desire of the sovereign to comprehend the wisdom of the Three Kings pleases me above all his riches and the magnificence of his palace,' replied Confucius. 'Just as the rank of Lord of Ten Thousand Chariots was not enough to satisfy the luxurious extravagance of the tyrants Jie of Xia and Zhou of Shang, so a kingdom of only a hundred leagues is not too small to be governed according to the wise precepts of the Emperors Yao and Shun. If the Duke Ling truly desires to put an end to the misfortunes of this world and strive honourably for the happiness of his people, I shall gladly lay my bones to rest in this land.'

Confucius and his disciples were ushered into the palace grounds by and by. Their black lacquered shoes clacked loudly against the polished stone of the floor, upon which not a single speck of dust lingered. Thus, they passed before a workshop, where many women were weaving brocade, their shuttles making a terrific noise and the women themselves singing in unison:

These most delicate feminine hands
Will surely sew the robes…

And from the shade of a peach grove, where the blossom resembled perfectly the brocade, issued the listless lowing of cattle in the royal pasture.

On the wise advice of Zhongshu Yu, the Duke Ling had asked his wife to retire with her attendants and purify her lips, which were yet imbued with the savour of fragrant liquors. Attired in robes befitting the solemnity of the occasion, the Duke welcomed Confucius in one of the many palace chambers and plied him with questions on the means by which to enrich his realm, strengthen his armies and become ruler of everything under heaven.

But to the sovereign's questions about war—which only harms a country and sacrifices the lives of its people—the Sage did not offer so much as a word in reply. Nor did he speak of the thirst for wealth—which only bleeds a people and robs them of their possessions. Instead, he solemnly preached the primacy of virtue over military victories and material gain. He made known the difference between the way of the conqueror who subjugates nations by force and that of the true sovereign who wins over the world with benevolence.

'If it is noble virtue that you truly seek, you must first vanquish your own desires.'

Such was the Sage's lesson.

From that day on, the heart of the Duke was no longer guided by the words of his wife but by those of the Sage. Every morning, in the Great Hall of the palace, he was taught the art of true government, while every evening, having climbed the Tower of Spirits, he learnt to read the movement of the celestial bodies according to the four divisions of time. He no longer visited his wife's bedchamber at night. The noise of the looms in the workshop was replaced by the whistles of bows, the echoes of hooves and the voice of the flute, for his noblemen were practising the Six Arts. Early one morning, when the Duke climbed alone to the top of the tower and looked over the parapet to survey his demesne, he saw brightly feathered songbirds warbling in the fields and mountains, magnificent flowers adorning every house and peasants singing the praises of their lord and master as they headed out to plough. Hot tears of emotion welled in the Duke's eyes.

'Why are you crying like this?' he heard a voice ask suddenly.

At the same time, a sweet and captivating aroma teased his nose. It was the clove-fragranced Rooster's Tongue incense that Nanzi always held in her mouth, mingling with the perfume of the rosewater from the Western Regions with which her robes were forever doused. The enchanting spell of these aromas emanating from the long-neglected beauty threatened to pierce the jade serenity of the Duke's thoughts with sharp, cruel claws.

'I implore you,' the Duke replied. 'Do not search my eyes with that mysterious gaze of yours. Do not enfold my body in your arms. Though the Sage has taught me to overcome evil, I know not yet how to resist the power of beauty.'

With that, brushing aside his wife's hand, the Duke turned away.

'Ah, this Kong Qiu has wasted no time in stealing you away from me. It is only natural that I should have stopped loving you a long time ago, but that does not give you the right to stop loving me.'

A furious rage inflamed Nanzi's lips. In the days before her alliance with the Duke, she had taken a lover by the name of Song Zhao, a young nobleman from the state of Song, so her wrath was not due to the cooling of her husband's affections now, so much as it was to her loss of power over his heart and mind.

'It is not that I do not love you,' the Duke replied. 'I wish to love you as a man should love his wife. But until now, I have served you as a slave does his master and revered you as a man does a goddess. I have sacrificed my country and my people, my fortune and my life to you: such have I toiled to satisfy your pleasures. But through the Sage's words, I have come to know that there are nobler deeds. Before, I drew the best of my strength from the beauty of your flesh. But now, the wisdom of the Sage has inspired in me an even greater might.'

As he told her of his courageous resolve, the Duke spontaneously raised his head and came face to face with the wrathful countenance of his wife.

'You wouldn't have the boldness to go against my word,' she said. 'Truly, you are a wretched creature. No man on earth merits greater pity than he who has no will of his own. But I shall wrest you from the clutches of Confucius forthwith. Though your tongue may have spoken some very fine words just now, are not your eyes already fixed on me with rapture? I can steal the soul of any man. You'll see soon enough: that Sage, that Confucius, will be in my power.'

With these words, glancing sidelong at the Duke, a triumphant smile upon her lips, Nanzi left the tower, her long robes rustling noisily behind her.

The Duke's heart, in which until that day serenity had reigned, was suddenly and cruelly cleft with division.

'Of all the men of quality who come from the four horizons to the state of Wei, there is not one who would not first seek an audience with me. The Sage, it is said, sees great value in etiquette, so why is it that he does not present himself?'

When the eunuch Yong Qu conveyed his mistress's words to the Sage, Confucius' modesty forbade him to demur.

Attended by his disciples, Confucius presented himself at the palace. Facing north, they prostrated themselves respectfully before Nanzi's throne; from behind a screen of brocade drapes, the tips of the consort's embroidered slippers were just visible. As she bowed her head to greet her guests, a heavy clatter of gemstones in the pendants of her necklace and bracelets rang out.

'Whosoever, having visited the state of Wei, has set eyes upon my face has raved: "Her Serene Highness has the brow of Daji and the eyes of Baosi." If you truly are a sage, then tell me whether a more beautiful woman has graced the earth since the times of the Three Sovereigns and Five Emperors.'

With these words, the consort threw aside the drapes and, with a cheerful laugh, bid Confucius and his disciples approach the throne. Arrayed in a phoenix crown with gold hairpins and hawksbill combs, enswathed in robes of rainbow colours that glittered like the scales of a fish, Nanzi smiled, her face like the radiant disc of the sun.

'I have heard talk of those who have great virtue,' said Confucius. 'But of those who have great beauty, I know nothing.'

Nanzi tried once more:

'I collect every rarity and curiosity in this world. In my coffers I have both gold from Daqu and jade from Chuiji. In my gardens I have turtles from Luju and cranes from the Kunlun mountains. But no more have I seen the fabled seven holes in the heart of the righteous than I have the *qilin* that appeared at the Master's birth. If you truly are a sage, will you not show me these wonders?'

'I am not versed in rarities or curiosities,' Confucius replied severely, his face now altered. 'I have learnt only what is known or ought to be known by the common people.'

The sovereign's wife softened her tone.

'Many men have gazed upon my features and heard the music of my voice. In every case, their brows were thereby unfurrowed and the clouds lifted from their darkened faces. Why should it be, then, that the Master wears a look of dejection? To me, sorrowful countenances seem ever unsightly. I know a young man from the state of Song by the name Song Zhao: his brow is not as noble as yours, but his gaze is as radiant as the spring sky. I have, moreover, in my service a eunuch, Yong Qu: his voice may not have the solemnity of yours, but his tongue is light, like a bird of spring. If you truly are a sage, your face ought to be bright enough to match the generosity of your heart. Now I shall drive away the clouds of sorrow upon your brow and wipe away the troubled shadows that darken it.'

Turning to her attendants, she had a box brought to her.

'I have all kinds of incense. One has only to inhale their fragrance into a chest full of cares to be carried off into a land of dream and fantasy.'

With these words, seven ladies-in-waiting carrying aloft seven incense-burners, each wearing a golden crown and a sash adorned with a pattern of lotus blossoms, surrounded Confucius on all sides.

The consort opened the incense box and threw various joss sticks, one by one, into the censers. Seven pillars of heavy smoke rose lazily up the curtains embroidered with gold threads. Yellow, lilac and whitish clouds of sandalwood filled the room with mysterious dreams that had for centuries lain at the bottom of the South Seas. The perfume of twelve varieties of tulip locked in all the vigour of fragrant herbs nurtured by the spring mists. The ambergris that is the thickened and hardened saliva of the dragons inhabiting the swamps at Daishikou, the agarwood extracted from the root of the lign-aloes that grow in Jiaozhou—both are possessed of the power to lead men's souls to distant worlds of sweet reverie. But the Sage's face only darkened.

'Ah, at last your face is brightening up,' said Nanzi with a radiant smile. 'I have all manner of wines that I serve in the rarest of cups. Just as the smoke of the incense has poured sweet nectar into the bitterness of your soul, so shall a few drops of wine bestow a merry ease on the severity of your flesh.'

With these words, seven ladies-in-waiting, each wearing a silver crown and a sash adorned with a pattern of Malabar plums, deferentially set an array of wines and vessels atop a table.

The consort picked up the splendid cups one by one and, having filled them with wine, offered them to her guests. These exquisite elixirs had the strange power of rousing contempt for proper values and inspiring an exclusive love of beauty. One of them, poured into a goblet of azure jasper, which cast cerulean reflections, was like a sweet, heavenly dew that granted celestial pleasures forbidden to mere mortals. The second cup, as thin as paper and the colour of green jade, had a curious property: no sooner was the cold wine poured into it than it began to bubble, all the better to warm the belly of the most forlorn guest. A third cup was made from the head of a crustacean found in the South Seas, with fearsome red antennae several feet long; it was encrusted with droplets of gold and silver, which gave the impression of the spray of waves. But the Sage's brow only furrowed.

'Your face is brightening and brightening,' said Nanzi with an ever more radiant smile. 'I have all manner of fowl and game. Those who, thanks to the fragrance of incense, have cleansed their souls of all cares, and who, thanks to the power of these libations, have freed their bodies of all tension, must cultivate their palates with rich nourishment.'

With these words, seven ladies-in-waiting, each wearing a crown encrusted with pearls and a sash adorned with a pattern of silver grasses, bore in several dishes arrayed with all manner of fowl and game and set them upon the table.

The hostess then bid her guests to sample the dishes one by one. Among them was the womb of a black panther, Danxue chicks, dried dragon meat from the Kunshan mountains, and elephant's foot. One had only to taste these exquisite meats for all thought of good and evil to vanish from one's heart. But the clouds did not lift from the Sage's face.

'Ah, how your bearing grows more noble, how your features grow ever more in their splendour,' said Nanzi for the third time, beaming. 'Whosoever has inhaled these marvellous perfumes, imbibed these sharp and potent wines, partaken of these rich and fatty meats shall live in a world of such intoxicating beauty, undreamt of by ordinary mortals, a world so violent and intense, where they can escape the cares and sorrows of this life. This is the world that I shall now unveil before your very eyes.'

Having spoken thus, she turned to a eunuch in her retinue and pointed to something behind a curtain that partitioned the front of the chamber. The deep folds of the heavy brocade then parted at the centre to reveal a staircase leading down to a garden. At the bottom, upon a carpet of green and fragrant grass, bathed in the warm light of the spring sun, a swarm of innumerable creatures, some looking up at the heavens, some squatting low to the ground, some leaping about, fighting even, crawled, swarmed, and piled on top of one another. From this motley host there came a terrific clamour: cries, high and piercing, mixed with groaning, deep and anguished. Some of the figures were soaked in crimson, like peonies in full bloom, while others quivered like wounded doves. It was a crowd of the damned in the midst of cruel tortures, as many for their transgression of the severe laws of the land as to delight the eyes of the consort. Each of them had been stripped of his clothes, and not one had his flesh intact. For the merest mention of the consort's vices, men had been disfigured with hot irons, their necks chained, and their ears gouged. There were also beauties who, for having attracted the attention of the Duke and thus incurred the envy of his consort, had had their noses cut off, both their legs amputated or been clapped in irons. Plunged by the spectacle into a state of rapture, Nanzi's countenance had both the beauty of a poet and the solemnity of a philosopher.

'From time to time the Duke and I ride through the streets of our capital. If the Duke should happen to cast a flirtatious look at a passing girl, I never fail to arrest her, and this is the fate that awaits. How would you like to take a ride through the city with us today? Having seen these punishments, would you dare to contradict my desires?'

There lurked in these words such power as could crush a man. To speak such cruelties with a look of tenderness was her custom.

On a certain day in the spring of the year 493 before the birth of Christ, two four-horse carriages were passing through the streets of the capital of Wei, which stands upon the ruins of the city of Yin between the Yellow and the Jishui rivers. In the first, shaded by parasols carried by two female attendants and escorted by a great many high officials and ladies of the court, rode, alongside the Duke Ling of Wei and the eunuch Yong Qu, the Duke's consort Nanzi, emulator of Daji and Baosi. In the other, accompanied by his disciples, was the Sage Confucius, emulator of Yao and Shun, who himself hailed from the wilds of Zou.

'Ah, how plain it is to see that even the virtue of this Great Sage is no match for the tyranny of this woman. Once again it is her word that shall be the law in the state of Wei.'

'How mournful the Great Sage looks! And how triumphant the Duke's consort! Never has her beauty been so dazzling.'

Such were the words of the common people lining the streets as the procession passed.

That evening, the Duke's consort, having adorned her face with especial care, waited in her apartments, stretching out on her bed with its exquisite brocade, until late at night, when at last she heard the stealthy sound of footsteps and there came a gentle knock at the door.

'Ah, here you are at last,' she said. 'Never again will you escape my embraces.'

Reaching out her arms, she enfolded the Duke Ling in her long sleeves. Her supple arms, inflamed by wines, enchained him as though in fetters.

'I despise you,' said the Duke, his voice trembling. 'You are an evil woman, a devil who means to destroy me. And yet, no matter how I try, I cannot be parted from you.'

The woman's eyes sparkled with the pride of evil.

The very next morning, Confucius and his disciples took to the road once again to preach the Way in the state of Cao.

'I have not yet seen a man who loved virtue as zealously as he did pleasure.'

Such were the last words spoken by the Sage as he left the state of Wei. To this day, they are handed down to us in the venerable writings of the *Analects*.

KILLING O-TSUYA

1

I T WAS AROUND the tolling of the fifth hour, in the early evening, when Harugorō, a fishmonger from one of the back streets, came rushing into the Suruga-ya pawnshop in a flush of drink. Merrily jingling the large front pocket of his work apron, he extracted the freshly minted two-shu silver coin just given him, so he said, from an official serving in the coiners' guild in the Ginza, and, having handed it over, he recovered his spring clothes— a hanten and a haori—which had been languishing in pledge for a little over three months. After he left, however, possibly on account of the foul weather, not a single other customer parted the curtain at the entrance to the ordinarily busy pawnshop. From his perch behind the lattice of the counter, Shinsuke, who had been engrossed in a popular novel, his chin propped up on his hand, now tended to the dying embers of the brazier, grumbling to himself about the bitter cold. He then reached out a hand to clip the ear of the shop boy who was dozing soundly right beside him.

'Shōta! Hey, wake up! I know it's sleeting, but be a good lad and run over to the Old Hermitage, the soba house in Muramatsu-chō, and ask them to send over two bowls of tempura soba. Get something for yourself, too, if you like.'

'Now there's an idea! Seeing as I'm awake… It's cold, and I'm hungry, so why not let you treat me to something before the master returns?'

With these words, Shōta smartly tucked in the hem of his kimono, and, no sooner had he picked up the broad-brimmed hat that was lying on top of the geta box, than he dashed out into the sleeting blizzard.

After tidying up the counter and padlocking the door to the storeroom, Shinsuke shut the main entrance to the shop. The owner and his wife had gone out early that evening to visit some relatives in Yotsuya who had fallen on hard times. As he left, the owner had told Shinsuke that they would probably not return until very late, or even until the following morning, depending on the circumstances, and so he should be sure to close up properly. With the master's words ringing in his ears, Shinsuke set off, lantern in hand, to check all the doors, from the kitchen to the back yard, then upstairs, where the maids' quarters were, to check the storm shutters that opened onto a balcony that was used for drying laundry. As he made his way back downstairs, the light from the lantern dimly lit up the tops of two heads: servants who were asleep in the darkness, snug beneath their quilts with a design of arabesques.

'O-Tami? Are you asleep?' he ventured, raising his voice slightly. But there came no reply.

Then, trying to muffle the sound of his footsteps as best he could, he carried on, treading along the icy floorboards of the corridor, to check the door to the veranda that skirted the inner garden.

The light of a lamp made the sliding paper door of the eight-tatami room adjoining the veranda glow a pale red. Usually, the room, in which there stood a large rectangular brazier in front of a Buddhist altar, and beside it a chest where the tea things were kept, was reserved for the owners. That night, however, taking advantage of their absence, the daughter of the house, O-Tsuya, appeared to have ensconced herself there.

Suddenly gripped by a keen sense of anguish and regret for his lowly status, Shinsuke thought how cosy it must be in there, as he gazed enviously at the flickering red light.

For more than a year already, he had been in love with O-Tsuya, who, for her part, was far from indifferent to him. Yet, no matter how much they might have loved one another, she, being the owner's only daughter, was well beyond Shinsuke's reach.

Had I been born to a great family and not that of a pauper, he lamented in his heart, I could have asked for the beautiful O-Tsuya's hand in marriage…

It must have been close upon midnight. The bitter cold had stolen into the house, and Shinsuke, as he loitered in the corridor, was shivering on account of the draught blowing in through the gap in the door. He passed the lantern to his left hand, which he had been keeping warm inside the breast of his kimono, and began to blow on the numb fingertips of the other. When they touched, his thighs were so cold that they no longer seemed to be a part of his body. Yet the cold was hardly the only thing sending shivers running through him.

'Shinsuke, is that you?' O-Tsuya called out to him.

She must have woken up just as he was passing by the tatami room—unless, of course, she had been awake all along. She seemed to have moved the shade of the night light as well, turning it towards the corridor, for the shoji now glowed a more intense red than before.

'Yes, it's me,' he said. 'The master won't be back until late, so I've been going around checking that the doors are all shut.'

'Are you turning in now, too?'

'Chance would be a fine thing! I have to stay up until the master comes back.'

As Shinsuke knelt there, placing both of his hands on the floor and bowing in an attitude of deference to the daughter of the house, the shoji was suddenly pulled back from inside the room, creating a gap about a foot wide.

'It's cold out there. Come in and close the screen behind you,' said O-Tsuya, as she combed up a stray hair at her temple. She was sitting amid her Gunnai silk quilts, her long-lashed gaze fixed in adoration upon the man who, even in the dim light, looked fair and handsome.

'Everyone else has gone to bed, I suppose?'

'No, I sent young Shōta out on an errand, and he should be back any minute. As soon as he returns, I'll send him straight to bed, so if you could just wait a little longer till then...'

'All this waiting and waiting... How tiresome it is! Opportune nights like this are such a rarity. Come on, Shinsuke, tonight of all nights, isn't it time to make up your mind?'

Dressed in a night robe of dappled scarlet, its fabric as supple as water, O-Tsuya rearranged her two alabaster feet, which peeked out from under the quilt, and placed her hands together in a gesture of supplication.

'Make up my mind? What on earth do you mean?'

Under the onslaught of all this beauty that seemed to snatch his breath away, Shinsuke lifted his gaze in a

45

wide-eyed stare that was, for all his twenty years, much too innocent and naïve. The sight made his heart pound like never before.

'Run away with me tonight! We'll go to Fukagawa. There's no use talking about it any more. See how I'm begging you!'

'Impossible!' he spluttered, worrying how he would manage to keep his iron resolve in the face of such bewitching allure. Ever since the age of fourteen, when he was taken on as an apprentice in the pawnshop, he had served so faultlessly that the master placed such faith in this boy as he would in no other. If he could just wait another year or two, he may not be able to marry the fragrant, charming O-Tsuya, but the master would surely set him up in business, and then he would be well on his way to all the fortune and success that one could wish for. What a joy this would be for his old parents, who were living in the Kiyoshima neighbourhood of Asakusa in the hope and expectation of this glad day. The idea of seducing and eloping with a young woman—his master's daughter, no less—was preposterous; he could not, must not do it, he told himself over and again.

'So, you've forgotten the promise you made to me just the other day? Well, have you, Shinsuke? Yes, now I see it all. You mean to make a plaything of me, so that you can cast me aside when you're finished. It's as plain to see as day.'

'Nothing of the kind… It's just—'

He was about to place a comforting hand on O-Tsuya's shoulder, which was heaving as she attempted to stifle her sobs, when suddenly there came a loud and insistent rapping at the front door. Taken aback by Shōta's return, Shinsuke flew into a panic, hastily grabbing his lantern and leaping to his feet.

'I'll come back later, I promise, once Shōta has gone to bed, and we'll talk it over. If you really are serious about this, I'll have to give it some thought…'

Having at last disengaged himself from O-Tsuya's embrace, Shinsuke returned to the shop, his composure regained, and hastened to unlock the side door.

'Oh, I'm frozen!' cried the youth as he rushed in, practically tumbling onto the dirt floor. 'It's started snowing out there, Shinsuke!' he said, brushing the snow off his broad-brimmed hat. 'It looks like we're in for some heavy snowfall tonight.'

It was about an hour later when the young apprentice, having finished off his part of the midnight repast, crawled into bed and fell asleep. The wind had abated, unnoticed, but the snow was evidently still falling, for a deathly stillness had settled outside in the sleeping streets. Shinsuke went to fetch a few lumps of cherrywood charcoal from the coal bunker under the kitchen floor, placed them in the brazier, and then, wearing a look of dejection, crouched all by himself in a corner of the shop. As he did so, he knew that the daughter of the house would be waiting for him in the back, with no thought of sleep; with that notion and others racing through his mind, he felt that the hour of his fate—a fate that would surely determine the rest of his days—was coming fast upon him. If only the owner would make haste and return, he thought, then this terrible temptation would simply vanish of its own accord.

When he heard the faint sound of the shoji being slid open in the back room, followed by what seemed to be stealthy steps along the veranda, Shinsuke leapt to his feet and once again, with muffled footsteps, stole towards the girl's bedchamber. He did this, realizing the disaster that would ensue if the impatient young mistress began calling out for him. The two of them found one another just at the corner of the corridor, in front of the lavatory.

'Are you ready, Shinsuke? I've brought enough money to see us through for a little while. Here, take this purse and look after it.'

O-Tsuya thrust both her hands under the folds of her kimono, making her breast swell under the black satin collar, and, from the depths of her bosom, she extracted a purse of saffron-coloured cloth, which she pressed into his hands. Judging by its weight, it must have held about ten ryo.

'Not only to run off with the master's daughter, but to steal his money into the bargain!… Heaven will see to it that I pay dearly for this.'

Though he spoke these words, Shinsuke put up no resistance and took the money from her.

'What a pity it seems to be snowing outside, though… I shouldn't mind it, of course, but you'd be frozen to death if you were to go all the way to Fukagawa in this dreadful weather. Besides, if we don't do it this evening, there will be other opportunities.'

In speaking of Fukagawa, they had in mind a certain boathouse in the Takabashi neighbourhood. There was a boatman there, by the name of Seiji, who had patronized the Suruga-ya pawnbroker's for a good decade at least. Having hired out boats for clam-gathering picnics at the sandbars around Shinagawa and for the yearly festivities marking the start of the boating season at Ryōgoku, he had come to know both O-Tsuya and Shinsuke well. Aside from paying his respects at O-Bon and the New Year, Seiji was wont to drop by the pawnbroker's kitchen every now and then to admire O-Tsuya's beauty over a cup of sake.

'Say what you like,' he would begin, 'but when it comes to O-Tsuya here, she's certainly the belle of Tachibana-chō!… You won't find another as beautiful as she in all Edo. I really shouldn't say this, but if O-Tsuya were a geisha… After all, I've still a ways to go before I turn fifty!… Well, who wouldn't want to hire her?'

As he rambled on in this droll fashion, he would occasionally take hold of O-Tsuya's sleeve, saying, much to the mirth of the household, 'Now you be a good girl, O-Tsuya, and just sit yourself down here beside me. Grant old Seiji his life's wish and pour him a cup of sake with your own fair hands. I don't ask for much. Just a cup. A single, solitary cup will do!…'

Taxiing people to and fro between Yanagibashi, Fukagawa and San'ya, Seiji was immersed in the atmosphere of the pleasure quarters and was worldly enough to see the love that the girl and Shinsuke had hidden from public view for so long. Yet, for a man so given to gossiping, he had done well to hold his tongue and had never yet breathed a word of it to anyone. The first time he ever came out with this knowledge was at the end of the previous month, when he dropped by unexpectedly after a trip to Yanagibashi. That day, O-Tsuya had been invited by her parents to join them at the theatre, but, not wanting to miss an opportunity to be alone with Shinsuke, who was to be left in charge of the shop, she feigned illness and stayed at home to convalesce. Early that morning her parents left, taking two of the maids with them, since it would be a pity, they reasoned, to leave them behind on account of O-Tsuya alone. In reality, however, it was Shōta who saw to the customers, for Shinsuke spent most of his time by O-Tsuya's bedside. When Seiji arrived, he poked his head in, his face flushed with drink. Seeing them, he made an insinuating little noise and, with a smirk, went to slap Shinsuke on the back.

'You're getting awfully cosy there, aren't you, Shinsuke?' he said. 'Thought nobody knew, did you? I've had my eye on your little intrigue for long enough. The world is full of blind people, but you can't pull the wool over old Seiji's eyes, oh no. Don't you worry, though, I won't let the cat out of the bag. So you might as well drop the act. And who knows… If you do, I might just be of some help to you. Besides, it's only natural when you find a beauty like O-Tsuya and a play-actor like yourself thrown together under one roof. I may have strange notions, but whenever I see a young couple such as yourselves in trouble, I always try to fix things. I always want to go beyond the call of duty and do whatever I can to help.'

Caught off guard, the couple started and momentarily exchanged wary glances, but Seiji had fathomed everything well enough and was starting to get carried away.

'In love, nothing comes of being as timorous as all that. Why don't you tell old Seiji all about it rather than keeping it to yourselves? It'd be much simpler if I presented your case and tried to win over the master so that you could marry in the open. I'm not trying to fawn, but, Shinsuke, you're a good lad, done well for yourself, you've got a good head on you and have reasonable prospects. Surely the master wouldn't object.'

'If that were possible, we should ask him ourselves without putting you to the trouble,' Shinsuke said, taking the bait and unwittingly explaining the situation in which they found themselves: seeing that O-Tsuya was the only daughter of the house, and he was his parents' only son, there was simply no way, no matter how they might try, that the two of them could be married.

'I'd rather kill myself than not be with you!' said O-Tsuya, collapsing in floods of tears after hearing out her beloved's account.

'Come now, dear lady,' said Seiji. 'Don't go upsetting yourself like that. I have just the solution, so take my advice. What we're going to do is stage ourselves a little comedy: you're both going to run away from here and come and stay with me. Then, I'll take matters in hand and smooth things over with your families. Just you wait and see how well things turn out.'

The young lovers had in fact talked of eloping earlier that very evening, and so, emboldened now by Seiji's suggestion, O-Tsuya had immediately been won over by the prospect. Shinsuke, meanwhile, was undecided.

'Surely you don't mean to refuse me now!'

As she spoke, O-Tsuya clasped the wrists of the young man, who stood there passively, dejectedly, his arms folded and his head slumped. She leant over, like a length of bamboo under a heavy weight, and pressed him, threatening and shaking him.

'If you refuse, I'll die! Die!'

'What choice do I have?… If that's how it is, if there's no other way, we'll do it, just as you say.'

Shinsuke quickly ran back to the shop to find his wicker clothes box. Opening it, he pulled out a heavy cotton kimono with thin vertical stripes and traded it with the one he had on. This heavier one had been cut from an old kimono of his father's; it was the only garment that had not been given him during his time as an apprentice and, as such, was the only one he believed he had any right to take with him. Then, going over to the shoebox by the side entrance, he stealthily picked out O-Tsuya's pair of black lacquered geta, which he hugged tightly under his arm as though treasuring them.

Having made his way back to the veranda, he found her standing there, waiting, arrayed in a kimono of yellow silk with a pattern of darker criss-crossing stripes, her embroidered satin obi fastened high on her chest, her hair done up in a shimada coiffure, her feet bared because she, who had always emulated the style of geisha, declined to wear tabi. He was almost aghast to think that she might run away so scantily apparelled in such bitter cold.

'Come on, then! This way,' said Shinsuke, who had slid open the rain door closest to the veranda by a few feet and hopped down into the inner garden. There, under the few inches of snow that had already fallen silently, everything—the hedges, the shrubs, even the wood panelling of the lavatory—was covered in white, as though an ermine mantle had been spread over it. Guided by the snowy light alone, the young man groped for O-Tsuya's heels as she sat over the edge of the veranda and placed her soft but icy soles against the lacquered boards of the geta. With hearts pounding as the snow crunched gently under their every step, the two lovers stole out through the back gate into the open street as stealthily as possible.

The sky was clouded over and pitch black, but the snow was not as heavy now, a few large flakes still fluttering down, and it was milder than they had expected. Under a single oil-paper umbrella with a bull's-eye design, they made their way from Tachibana-chō towards Hama-chō, the girl holding the handle, the young man's hand clasped over hers.

The slender lines of Shinsuke's figure belied his true nature, for the youth was tall, sinewy and of above average strength. In the grip of surging emotions, he would suddenly clench his fist with such terrible force that O-Tsuya's delicate hand, half numb from the cold, seemed to risk being crushed. Every so often she would cry out in pain and ask whether something was the matter, her eyes full of concern. Even in the dark, he could see their long, narrow slits glittering brightly.

As they were crossing the Shin-Ōhashi bridge, a bell rang out the eight strokes of deepest night. Its tolling echoed towards the great Sumida river at high tide, as though commanding the waters, too, to roar and bellow, although they were dead from having swallowed so much snow.

'What a lovely sound that bell makes! It's just as if we were in a play,' said O-Tsuya, who until that point had hardly spoken.

'Your optimism is a thing of wonder, O-Tsuya,' Shinsuke replied with a grimace.

And with that, the two lovers carried on their way in silence until they had arrived safely at the boatman's house, perched on the bank of the Onagi canal.

2

'T O SETTLE IT ALL right and proper, we can't afford to rush things, you know. Ten days or so should do the trick. In the meantime, you had better stay out of sight as much as possible. The rooms upstairs are at your disposal—you can amuse yourselves all you like up there.'

Thus, seeing to their every need and comfort, did Seiji welcome them, instructing his wife and staff to do likewise. However, ten days turned into a fortnight, and still no glad tidings came from the boatman.

'I know that Seiji is a busy man,' Shinsuke was wont to say, 'but isn't it also possible that things haven't turned out quite the way he'd hoped and that's why he's keeping us in the dark?'

Little by little, Shinsuke had begun to worry like this, but O-Tsuya was far more sanguine about the situation.

'You shouldn't go upsetting yourself like that,' she would reply. 'Now that we've eloped, what difference does it make? After all, if it doesn't work out, we can still live together even without their permission… I've never been so happy in all my life, so I really haven't the slightest urge to go home.'

Ever since arriving in her new abode, O-Tsuya had become a totally different person. She was gayer and more reckless. The window of their upstairs apartment gave directly onto the stone bank of the narrow canal, which flowed down towards the Sumida river; every day, boats from Naka-chō, Ishiba, Yagurashita, Otabi, Benten and other pleasure quarters, each carrying with them geisha and their sophisticated clientele, would moor there, and so it was not uncommon for the young couple to hear, through the thin fusuma separating them from the neighbouring quarters, the sweet nothings being whispered by the parties who had taken rooms there.

Carefully observing the geisha, O-Tsuya had quickly mastered their ways, and, a few days after her arrival, she replaced the pretty shimada-style chignon that she had worn when leaving her parents' house with a more manageable Hyōgo knot, adorning her abundant hair with boxwood combs elegantly placed above the temples. She had donned a padded house kimono cut from a garish cloth that the boatman's wife had offered her against the cold, and the habit of smoking uninhibitedly now crowned her attempt to imitate what was commonly thought to be the at-home manners of a geisha. She had also picked up some words and phrases from the vernacular of these women, and, when she dropped them into conversation once or twice, Shinsuke frowned, wondering where on earth she had learnt to speak like that.

'Why are you so keen to imitate those wretches?' he said haughtily. 'Never in all my days have I bought a girl.'

Indeed, were it not for O-Tsuya, he might have been able to lead a decent and respectable life. Yet the girl scarcely paid any mind to his opinions. Her newfound situation had so completely carried her away that now, overbrimming with joy, she would laugh from morning till night and indulge all the extravagances that came into her head, demanding eels and game birds for every meal of the day, and even entertaining all the members of the household, right down to the hired boatmen, several times a week. Every evening, with a yet inexperienced hand, she would hold out her cup to be filled from the jugs of Kenbishi that Seiji, as an attentive host, never failed to place on his table, and she would drink down great gulps of the warm sake, emptying her cup each time. Some nights she would be so badly affected by drink, and her face would burn with such passion, that it led Shinsuke to wonder whether she were not mad; then she would writhe and wallow, her body aflame, giving him no sleep throughout the night. Helplessly, the two lovers were swept along in a torrent of pleasures so intense that it threatened to blot out their very existence.

So time wore on. The New Year's celebrations were fast approaching, and the market at the Hachiman shrine, which took place on the fifteenth of the month, was already behind them. But still the young couple received no word.

'I'm in the very midst of the negotiations with your parents,' the boatman would say. 'If you could just hold tight for another four or five days…' Such was his eternal refrain, uttered with a drawn look of sincere sorrow, whenever he saw the couple and was asked to account for the delay.

'Seiji, what wrong I've done to the master is truly inexcusable, but what's done is done. If it can't be helped, then so be it. We are prepared to set up a home of our own. I'm not one to act rashly, so can't you please just tell me how things really stand? After all, how much longer can we go on living off your kindness?'

Such appeals, however, would always be met with a benevolent laugh.

'Come now! You mustn't stand on ceremony with old Seiji! Besides, if the negotiations were really going nowhere, I'd have washed my hands of it once and for all. But I've already been over there half a dozen times! I've told them what's what so often that, between you and me, they've both practically agreed to give their blessing. You see, I keep telling them that it makes no sense for parents to refuse children who are so madly in love that they're prepared to run away. I gave them my word: until they say yes, you'll have a roof over your head and be taken care of here. So, as you can see,' he added airily, 'you really have no need to worry.'

Shinsuke anticipated that all this would be resolved before the year was out. After all, however difficult their situation might be, it would be inauspicious not to have things settled before the hustle and bustle of the New Year's celebrations. And so, he sincerely looked forward to the coming of spring.

The ten ryo of gold that O-Tsuya had brought with her had dwindled away on the girl's daily extravagances, and now not even half of it remained.

You can't well see out the year with only five ryo of gold, she thought to herself as she entrusted the hairdresser who came to the house with one of the silver hairpins that had adorned her shimada, so that she could have it discreetly exchanged for currency. And so, on the evening of the seventeenth, while the Mino Fair was taking place in Asakusa, she made a display of her largesse by having three pieces of gold distributed among the household staff as an end-of-year gift.

A little after sunset three days later, just as the couple were sitting down to their evening meal, Sōta, one of the hired hands, came tearing up the stairs. 'Here's something that'll put a smile on your face, Shinsuke,' he said. 'Right this minute, the boss is having a talk with your old man at Kawa-chō, up in Yanagibashi. He's sure it's all going to be tied up at last, so he told me to get you in a boat and to take you over there right away. Only, since it might be a little awkward having you and the young miss there together, I'm sorry to say he's told me to leave her here. You don't mind, do you, O-Tsuya? Besides, Shinsuke doesn't want you clinging to his sleeves day and night. A little break of an evening won't incur the wrath of heaven, after all.'

'Be that as it may, I still can't help worrying,' replied O-Tsuya, crestfallen.

A sudden change had come over her face. This was welcome news, to be sure. But then again… who could say? Perhaps Shinsuke would be taken back under the paternal roof in Asakusa. The thought struck fear in her. The hour they had long looked forward to was finally upon them, but now that it was here, the young man found himself assailed by similar doubts. For one thing, he had committed a terrible crime, and until he had obtained the forgiveness of his employer, how could he dare to show his face before his own father without blushing? It was this prospect that troubled him above all else. Pressed by Sōta to hurry, Shinsuke steeled himself and, having thrown his things together, raced down the stairs.

Alarmed by all this, O-Tsuya immediately rushed after him. Just as the two men were about to step onto the boat, she caught them by the sleeves.

'Wait! I don't mean to sound mistrustful, Sōta-san, but I just can't help worrying. Won't you please take me with you? I promise not to cause you any trouble.'

'What's all this? Oh, come off it, dear lady!' said Sōta, roaring with laughter as he jumped aboard the barge and set about undoing the mooring lines. 'You really are acting like a spoilt child. No trouble, my foot!… We aren't going to gobble him up, you know! You just trust the boss and everything will turn out all right. Why, your very being there could upset the negotiations.'

'But if that's what you're worried about, I can hide in a corner where they won't see me. Oh, please, I'm begging you: take me with you! I don't know why, but this evening especially, I can't bear the thought of letting Shinsuke go.'

O-Tsuya deftly extracted a gold coin from the folds of her obi and pressed it into the boatman's palm.

'Please, Sōta, couldn't you do it, just this once?'

'You were kind enough to give me money only the other day, miss… If you keep it up, I'll be the one who gets a telling off from the boss.'

Contrary to his usual habit, Sōta returned the coin with an air of embarrassment. Since he was the most influential of all the young lads in Seiji's employ, O-Tsuya had always treated him especially well, so it was now all the more wounding that he had refused her request out of hand.

'I'm touched by your concern,' said Shinsuke, 'but it's true that if we take you, we might embarrass Seiji, who's already done so much for us. I'd never forgive myself.'

Although he tried to console her like this, his face was awash with an uncanny pallor, and, as he stood by the water's edge in the half-light of dusk, his shoulders were trembling.

'In that case,' she began, 'you must promise me that if there's the least problem, you'll come back and see me first.'

'All right, all right,' said Shinsuke, nodding vigorously. 'Although, I doubt there's any cause to worry.'

He ought to have been overjoyed, for that evening his long-cherished dream was about to come true, but instead he felt as if he were on the verge of tears. He even found himself wondering whether it wouldn't be easier to take O-Tsuya and run off again somewhere.

From mid-morning that day, a southerly wind, so unusual in winter, had been blowing in, bringing with it a curiously warm air. From the moment she woke, O-Tsuya had complained of dizziness, and had applied a balm to her temples. Now, after all this haranguing with Sōta, tears of frustration welled in her eyes, so much that she was overcome by the heavy languor of her half-illness. Propping herself up against the frame of the upstairs window, she watched as the boat moved off, her eyes swollen from crying.

The moon had not yet risen that evening, and the clouds steadily gathering behind the watchtower on the Shin-Ōhashi bridge eventually filled half of a perfectly black sky, enswathing everything in the heavy curtain of night. In the twinkling of an eye, Sōta's swift little boat vanished into the deep mists of the river.

Leaving the mouth of the Onagi behind, the boat carried on into the great Sumida river. As it reached the midpoint, Shinsuke glanced with a heavy heart at the red-glowing bowl of his pipe, the only bright spot amid all the immeasurable darkness.

'What a filthy evening,' he said, as though to himself. 'We're in for some rotten weather tomorrow.'

'I just hope the rain holds off until nightfall,' said Sōta. 'By the looks of it, though, that might be wishful thinking. As soon as the wind dies down, there's sure to be a downpour.'

Sōta now exchanged his pole for a pair of oars, whose rhythmic creaking seemed to tease the water lapping at the gunwale before drifting off across its surface.

'Maybe I was a little harsh on O-Tsuya,' Sōta continued. 'The poor thing! Doubtless by now she'll be drowning her sorrows in a jug of sake.'

In those days, the Kawa-chō teahouse in Yanagibashi was a well-known establishment, and Shinsuke even recalled having gone there two or three times as part of his master's retinue when he was working in Tachibana-chō. Sōta seemed to be a familiar face there, and, flirting with the serving girls that he ran into as he made his way along the corridor, he would embarrass Shinsuke, saying things like, 'This evening I've brought a handsome young man for you—the spitting image of Mitsugorō!'

The two men were shown to a room looking out over the river, a tearoom decorated in refined and elegant taste, where they found Seiji waiting alone, leaning back against the alcove post, his face enlivened with a mellow flush of drink.

'What a pity,' he said, seeing the pair of faces. 'Your father was here only a moment ago, but he had to leave. I'm sorry, Shinsuke, but then you were so very late in coming.'

He then let out a disappointed sigh, his face betraying uncharacteristic chagrin.

Sōta, however, offered up an array of justifications, telling him how O-Tsuya had so obstinately intervened, delaying their departure. Hearing all this, Seiji let out a hearty laugh and instantly recovered his good humour. At the same time, freed from the onerous prospect of coming face to face with his father, and having the fear of being forced to return to Asakusa dispelled, Shinsuke regained his spirits.

'Well, seeing as you've come, you might as well stay for a drink,' said Seiji, pouring Shinsuke a cup of sake and proceeding to tell him all about the meeting with his father. Having taken a fare to the Tagawa-ya tcahousc in Daion-ji-mae earlier that evening, Seiji had taken advantage of the opportunity to call in at his father's house in Kiyoshima-chō and bring him there, where once again he had gone over everything with the old man and thrashed it all out. Shinsuke's father had said that it would be difficult to forgive the outrageous actions of a son who had seduced his master's daughter, but he conceded that if this were to cause the two lovers to run off for good, he would feel even guiltier vis-à-vis the owner of the Suruga-ya. And if, by some misfortune, it should end in the lovers' suicide, he was well aware that, whatever his own pain might be, the owner's house would be ruined by the irreplaceable loss of their only daughter. Even so, while such a rationale pushed him to relax the extreme rigidity of his position, he did not feel that he could justly give his consent without taking the girl's family into account. And so, the father had presumed to say only this: that if the owner of the Suruga-ya was prepared to let bygones be bygones, then he too was prepared to let his son marry into their family, even if this spelt the end of his own family line. In fact, if he had not had to contend with Seiji's good offices about the affair, he would surely, so Seiji said, have moved heaven and earth to track his son down and tear him to pieces. 'Just imagine how this makes me feel!' he had apparently said with manly tears welling in his eyes. Seiji had then comforted the stubborn old man as best he could, imploring him to forgive the young lad's misdeeds, if only for his own sake. He had said that if he was truly so disposed, there was every chance that the owner of the Suruga-ya, for his part, would also give his blessing. The conversation had gone well, and had carried on over a flask of sake, and Seiji, waiting for the right moment, finally suggested sending for Shinsuke, so that father and son might both be reassured. He advised that he teach the boy a lesson so that he might see the error of his ways. At first, the old man had refused, apparently deeming it inappropriate under the circumstances, but in the end he relented, consenting to Seiji's proposal. But since Shinsuke had taken so long in getting there, the old man, busy as he always was, especially with all the preparations for New Year's Eve, could be detained no longer and, having waited as long as he could, had just this minute left.

'See, Shinsuke, parents aren't so unforgiving after all.'

As Seiji uttered these words, Shinsuke, overwhelmed by a profound feeling of unworthiness, began to cry hot tears, his hands placed to the floor in supplication.

'Anyhow,' continued Seiji, 'we've been so wrapped up in this tale that our sake has gone cold. Come now, tonight we should cut loose and celebrate. Really, I should send for a geisha, but with such a fine-looking lad like you around, you never know: she might fall for you!'

Seiji kept pressing Shinsuke to drink, offering him prodigious amounts of sake. The young man was not especially fond of alcohol, but, perhaps on account of his robust constitution, no matter how much he drank, he had never yet been made ill by it, and so, casting off his melancholy, he graciously accepted the cups that were handed him in rapid succession.

By now, the sky was completely clouded over, just as Sōta had predicted, and no sooner had the wind dropped than came the patter of large raindrops striking the eaves, followed immediately by a violent downpour. A real deluge had begun, blending the sky and the river into one. The terrific din drowned out the voices of the three men, who, amid the fury of the elements that seemed to shake the little room in which they found themselves, carried on with their libations a while longer. The rain, however, gave no sign of abating.

'It's getting late,' said Seiji. 'I've got another piece of business to see to up in Koume, but I'll have quite a time of it in this weather.' Grumbling away, he clapped his hands loudly to call one of the serving girls. 'With your permission, Shinsuke, I'll go ahead in a palanquin, but you can have a quiet drink with Sōta here before you return home.'

With that, he got up and left.

The two young men stayed there another good hour, keeping an eye on the sky, but still the rain showed no sign of letting up. Shinsuke, moreover, began to worry about O-Tsuya, and in the end he declared that he would like to head back, even if it meant getting soaked. Sōta asked him whether he would like to go back by palanquin, since he had planned to leave the barge at a nearby boathouse and return on foot, but Shinsuke demurred, suggesting that they should walk together.

'Quite right,' agreed Sōta. 'It's only a short sprint to Takabashi. We can borrow an umbrella. Let's roll up our kimono and hot-foot it along the riverbank.'

Fortunately, the wind had died down completely. Having borrowed a lantern from the teahouse, Sōta headed out first, while Shinsuke followed on, dangling from a cord a wooden box filled with food that he had bought as a gift for O-Tsuya. Having tied the straps of their geta to their obi, they left the teahouse barefoot. Engulfed by darkness and torrential rain that prevented them from talking to one another, they were soaked through before they had made it even two or three blocks. At the far end of the Ryōgoku bridge, they turned right and, no sooner had they drawn up in front of the Lord Hosokawa's mansion than there came a gust of wind from the waterfront, extinguishing Sōta's lantern before he could even cry out. Little frequented at the best of times, the quayside, under this midnight deluge, was completely deserted, and there was no chance of finding a light. Without the lantern, the power of the darkness was even more terrifying: they felt as though they were being swallowed up, and even the sound of the rain seemed to assail their ears ever more violently.

'I know my way even in the dark, Shinsuke, but you ought to take care after that skinful you've had tonight!' Sōta bellowed.

True enough, Shinsuke had drunk close to three pints of sake. Both Sōta and Seiji had repeatedly asked how he was feeling, but he was in fact only slightly tipsy, and he could still stand well enough on his feet. Rather, it was he who felt anxious on Sōta's behalf.

'I'm just fine,' he replied, shouting as loud as he could. 'It's you I'm worried about!'

When no answer came, he supposed that the din of the rain had drowned him out.

A few moments later, after Shinsuke had taken another half-dozen or so steps, a figure suddenly appeared at the end of his nose, hurling abuse at him.

'Not another word out of you, you filthy drunk!'

In that instant, scarcely imagining his assailant to be Sōta, Shinsuke felt the icy tip of a blade slash the top of his shoulder. His reflexes were instantaneous, so the wound was only skin-deep, but the right side of his neck tingled all over, as though it had been clawed at by sharp nails, while one half of his face seemed to disappear, numb all of a sudden.

'Who the hell are you?' shouted Shinsuke, stumbling and preparing to flee.

'Too drunk to even recognize my voice, are you? I've brought you here to kill you. Boss's orders.'

With these words, Sōta rushed at him furiously. Shinsuke pressed his back firmly against the perimeter wall of the mansion and frantically brandished the handle of his umbrella. Twice or so he managed to repel his assailant, but soon enough the latter got past his guard and slashed him somewhere in the lower half of his body. To prevent Shinsuke's escape, Sōta pinned him to the wall, gripping the collar of his kimono with his left hand, while, with the other, he slashed at him, tearing the kimono to pieces. By now the two men were fighting frenziedly, both rolling around in the mud, punctuating their blows with insults and the cries of wild beasts. Mustering every last ounce of his strength, Shinsuke grabbed his assailant's right arm with both hands and twisted it as hard as he could, desperately trying to prise the weapon from his hand. Locked thus in this struggle to the death, Shinsuke was possessed by a strength and bravery that took him by surprise. Far too inebriated, Sōta was unable to withstand the brute force of his opponent's assault and at last relinquished the dagger. Still undaunted, however, he rushed at Shinsuke, but the latter immediately threw him to the ground and, launching himself astride his opponent, plunged the blade into the crown of his head, which grated against the bone, giving off a sound like a rat gnawing at it. In a flash, his body lay lifeless.

Why had he killed him? Why had he committed such an act of cruelty? He himself could not say. He remembered only feeling certain that if he hadn't killed him, he would not have had any hope of escape. It had all happened as though in a dream. Aside from the fact that he had received a psychological shock, and despite now having several serious wounds, his physical strength was so little depleted that he marvelled at the ease with which it was possible to kill a man. What to do now? Flee or turn himself in? The question immediately floated into his head, but he decided that the answer could wait until after he had seen O-Tsuya. The body of the boatman, which until moments earlier had been capable of laughter, anger and noise, was oddly silent, lying there like a piece of lumber, and, when he prodded it with the tips of his toes, it felt both frightening and ridiculous. Thus, he told himself, can a human being also be thought of as a devilishly ingenious machine. To prevent the crime from being discovered at once, he threw both the blade and the body into the river. Then, under the torrential rain that continued to fall violently, he made off in the direction of Takabashi as fast as his legs would carry him.

Sōta had said that his attempt to kill him was on the orders of the boss. In that case, unexpected though it was, Seiji had to be one of the worst kinds of criminals, and his boating business, no doubt, a front for a den of thieves. Killing him must have been a ploy to get his hands on O-Tsuya. Judging by the way in which he had left the teahouse, alluding to some business in Koume, O-Tsuya might well be in danger already. Besides, even if Seiji had yet to return home, his staff could be accomplices, and so, if they were conspiring against him, Shinsuke would have to be on his guard as he entered the house. At any rate, seeing O-Tsuya was not going to be easy. The more he mulled it all over, the more mortified he felt for having fallen into the trap set by this brute. Suddenly, the hatred and resentment he felt towards Seiji exploded all at once.

'To kill one man or two—what difference does it make? If the moment comes, I'll kill that bastard with my own hands, even if it means losing my own life in the process.'

Shinsuke began to plot recklessly and desperately, but he had to stay alive until he could see his beloved O-Tsuya. Imagining what he would do if he could not find her, he felt his heart swell with an inconsolable sorrow that drowned out even the hatred he had for Seiji.

Intent on penetrating the premises as stealthily as possible, Shinsuke, who had already begun to muffle his footsteps a few yards before he reached the building, turned into the side lane and pressed his ear to the storm shutters by the kitchen door, wondering whether he would hear O-Tsuya's crying, but the entire house seemed to be asleep, and he couldn't hear any voices at all. Since the dreadful weather was in his favour, he surmised that a little noise would not pose any great danger. The moment he laid hands on the corner shutter to prise it open, however, it slipped, probably having been left unfastened. A standing lantern dimly lit the rear tatami room, and there were no signs of anything especially untoward having happened. As a precaution, Shinsuke hid under the breast of his kimono the large carving knife that hung above the sink in the kitchen and tiptoed through to the foot of the stairs, when suddenly he heard the mistress of the house call out in hushed tones:

'Who's there? Is that you, Sōta?'

Shinsuke stopped dead in his tracks.

'Yes, it's me,' he replied in a voice as low and husky as hers.

'Did it go well, then?' she asked solicitously.

It sounded as though the mistress was alone, sitting beside the oblong brazier, cosy in her kotatsu and waiting impatiently for Sōta's return. Curiously, it so happened that evening, as if by chance, that none of the men who ordinarily slept in the large adjoining room was there. Had O-Tsuya been bundled off somewhere already, then? He felt a pang in his chest as he wondered.

'Don't worry. It went off without a hitch,' he said, mimicking Sōta's intonations, before sliding the shoji open and suddenly appearing before her eyes, standing there fearless. Then, carrying on with the same intonation, in a voice as restrained as it was terrifying, he asked where O-Tsuya was.

'Oh, it's you, Shinsuke!'

That was all the mistress could say, for she nearly fainted in surprise. While she searched for some means of subterfuge, Shinsuke was already bathed in an aura of murderous fury that seemed to forbid the slightest delaying tactic. He himself hadn't realized it until he saw himself by the light of the lantern, but with his clothes torn to pieces, soaked through, caked in mud and blood, he looked appalling, his appearance every bit that of some terrible demon. Breathing heavily, he knew now that there was no reason to hide his crime.

Having at last regained her composure, the mistress feigned innocence.

'Wondering what's happened, are you?' he said. 'I've killed Sōta: that's what's happened. But if you tell me where I can find O-Tsuya, I might just be convinced to spare your life.'

He brandished the knife menacingly under her nose, but she maintained her odious composure and, lighting her long pipe provocatively, replied that the young maiden was sure to be in her room upstairs.

A former prostitute who had served her term in the Yoshiwara district, she had replaced Seiji's first wife upon the latter's death. Although now a mature woman in her early thirties, she was still extremely attractive, with a wonderfully pale complexion and a shapely figure. She took great pride in her extraordinary strength of character, and it was precisely this almost masculine spirit that permitted her to meet the situation without flinching. She had, moreover, taken Shinsuke for nothing more than a tender, rather effeminate lover, so, even when he claimed responsibility for Sōta's murder, she supposed that he was merely saying this to frighten her and vowed not to show any sign of weakness.

Having decided to search the upper floor, Shinsuke set about tying the mistress up, hand and foot, so that she should not escape while he made his inspection.

'What fine manners!' she said, marvelling at his impudence.

Having taken him for a feeble creature, she threw herself back onto him, trying to knock him to the ground, but, in so doing, she received such an almighty blow to her back that she collapsed, half dead, in a heap, at the mercy of Shinsuke. His one and only experience in the matter had allowed him to master, with astonishing speed, the techniques required to break, twist, trample and crush a human body. Without any difficulty at all, he bound her arms and legs, and even went so far as to gag her.

Holding the lantern aloft, he proceeded upstairs, but no matter how he searched every nook and cranny—in the bedrooms, naturally, but also in the cupboards and behind the screens—O-Tsuya was nowhere to be found. Granted, he had expected this, but to see his fears confirmed brought him close to tears. A lost and helpless child, his heart bereft, he tore downstairs like a man possessed. Leaving no stone unturned, he now searched the rooms on the ground floor, even looking under the veranda—but, of course, to no avail.

'Well, what have you done with her?' he said, removing the gag. 'Come on, out with it! If you don't tell me, you'll answer for it with your life.'

He drew the flat of the knife smartly across the mistress's cheek, but she remained calm, her eyes closed, perfectly silent. Then, at last, she opened her eyelids and fixed Shinsuke in her gaze.

'Do you really think I can be intimidated by someone like you? A snivelling jackass still wet behind the ears! If you really mean to kill me, then be my guest. That's something I'd like to see.'

As she spoke these words, she closed her eyes again and sat there, as still as stone.

It suddenly occurred to him that he had forgotten about the maids' quarters. Thinking that he stood to discover more by threatening them than by striking this brazen woman, he rushed there only to find once again that, unaccountably, not one of the three maids lay asleep there. Doubtless, they had all been dispatched on various errands by the master and mistress, lest they disturb their crime.

Changing tack, Shinsuke once again returned to the mistress's side and abruptly untied the rope binding her hands and legs. Then, pressing his forehead to the tatami mat, his hands placed together in a beggar's act of supplication, he began imploring her feverishly:

'Oh, Mistress! I've wronged you! Forgive me, I pray you! For mercy's sake, don't be angry with me. Have pity! Only, please… won't you tell me where my O-Tsuya is? I beg of you! I beg of you!'

'You ought to know yourself whether or not she's here. After all, you've given the place such a thorough going-over. Her whereabouts isn't any of my business.'

'But why play the innocent now? What's the use? It doesn't take much to work out that you and your husband have connived to kidnap that young girl and take her away somewhere. Can't you see how straight I've been with you from the very start? Didn't I admit right away that I'd killed Sōta? I'm not talking about doing anything untoward to O-Tsuya after I find her; nor do I mean to track down your husband and revenge myself on him. I'd simply like to see my O-Tsuya one last time before I hand myself over to the authorities tomorrow. I can't bear to be parted from her without having said goodbye first. Won't you take pity on me? Even if I have cause to be angry with you, you certainly have none to hold a grudge against me. So why not grant me this last wish? I promise you that if you do, no matter what tortures the courts subject me to, I won't reveal anything that might incriminate you or your husband.'

'Now see here, Shinsuke. I've kept quiet long enough, listening to you prattle on with these wild theories and threats of incrimination, but what proof do you have? Taking somebody's life seems to have robbed you of your senses. As for Sōta, I've no idea what he might have been up to, but it certainly had nothing to do with us. So hand yourself in, take revenge, do what you like for all I care!'

'If you really are as blameless as you claim to be, then why won't you tell me where the girl is? And while we're at it, just where has that husband of yours got to?'

The woman was growing bolder by the minute.

'My husband?...' she replied in an icy tone, her arms folded haughtily. 'My husband goes out most evenings. You can't expect me to keep track of him all the time. As for O-Tsuya, she said she was going to the theatre this afternoon. She went out with the maids to the Hirokōji Avenue, but given it's so late and they aren't back yet, something must have happened.'

As he listened to this insolence, Shinsuke's mind once again took a terrible turn. 'You bitch!' he swore inwardly. 'What am I going to do with you?' If there really was no way of extracting O-Tsuya's whereabouts from the woman, he would have to delay turning himself in until he had found her, whether it took a month or even half a year. Would his crime go undetected in the meantime? The thought troubled him. There was one thing that he could count on, however: that this woman would make an anonymous report…

As he weighed up his situation, Shinsuke stood there for a long while, staring blankly at the profile of this shapely figure sitting there on the floor with one knee raised, puffing calmly on her pipe.

She is Seiji's wife, after all, he thought to himself. What if I were to kill her? That way, I wouldn't risk anything, and at the same time I'd avenge O-Tsuya. Just look at that brazen, defiant expression of hers… Sticking her nose in the air as though she's in control. Not in her wildest dreams does she think that I might kill her. How queer. All it would take is a sudden burst of strength to strangle her, and then she'd be little more than a corpse. Isn't it odd?

In an instant, he found himself once again drawn to violent impulses. Silent all the while, he picked up the length of rope lying at his feet, and, in a flash, so as to realize the act that he had just contemplated, he twisted it around the woman's neck.

The deed was done. What with all the strain he had been made to endure that day, he gave in to utter exhaustion. As he tried to conceive of himself as a callous criminal, it suddenly seemed to him that the pallor of his arms and legs had eerily darkened. He had to flee quickly, but he could not do so with his clothes soaked in blood. He went over to the back door, undressed and washed the blood off his body. By chance, he found there, on one of the shelves in the cupboard, a complete set of clothes—apparently having been laid out for Seiji to change into—and put them on. The clothes suited Shinsuke's rather sombre tastes: in addition to a wadded silk pongee and a haori, there was a stiff brown Hakata obi. Next, he opened one of the drawers in the cupboard and laid his hands on gold and silver coins worth some three ryo. This was, on the one hand, to replenish his own meagre purse, but also to create the impression of a burglary. As for the gaily coloured striped robes that he had been wearing, he weighed them down with the stone weight used for making pickled radishes and tossed them into the depths of the canal. Having thus dealt with the immediate evidence of his two murders, Shinsuke tried to quell his own sense of apprehension.

By now, the rain outside had stopped completely, and the cold light of the midnight moon was shining brightly in the clear sky. He donned a pale-gold headscarf bearing the family crest, which he had likewise stolen, and passed safely by the police box at the corner of the street leading into the main thoroughfare.

3

B ACK WHEN SHINSUKE had still been living with his parents in Asakusa, his father would often take him to see a relation of his, a professional gambler by the name of Kinzō, who lived in the Narihira quarter of the Honjō. It was there that Shinsuke, not knowing where else to turn on the night of his crimes, sought refuge. In his youth, Kinzō too had experienced episodes of violence, but since he had passed the milestone of fifty some two or three years prior, he had become, with the fortune that he had acquired alongside some good sense, a man of extreme moderation and such noble generosity and largesse rarely found in his profession. Certain that he could rely on a man like this without fear, Shinsuke gave him a broad outline of the story so far and, promising to hand himself over to the authorities as soon as he found O-Tsuya, begged Kinzō to shelter him in the meantime. However, while he had confessed to Sōta's murder, he decided to keep quiet about that of Seiji's wife.

'Now listen here, Shinsuke. I'm willing to hear you out, but there's something I just can't fathom. You say that you killed Sōta and fled the scene, coming straight here. But while your body's covered in wounds, your clothes are pristine. How on earth do you explain that, eh?'

Kinzō was quick to observe this. Caught out, Shinsuke began to tremble. As he left the boatman's house, he had believed that he had washed himself thoroughly enough, but Kinzō must have spotted the remnants of blood under his fingernails and around his neck, and that the hair above his left temple was caked in blood. In the end, with nowhere to hide, Shinsuke had no choice but to confess.

'Just as I suspected... But now that all that's been cleared up, I'll do what I can, and there's no reason why I shouldn't help you find that O-Tsuya, as you call her. Only, before we go any further, I must insist on one thing: that you promise to go and turn yourself in once you've found her. I, too, have killed once or twice in my time, and let me tell you: once you've developed a taste for it, it isn't easy to stop! You used to be a shy little thing, but that's certainly not the case any more. And when you have nothing left to fear in the world, everything becomes possible... You know, Shinsuke, this is a crucial moment for you. You have to get a grip and think clearly: if you don't give yourself up now, you'll be dragged down into the ways of evil, and then you'll become a real monster! I must seem heartless in telling you this, in telling you to go, whether you want to or not, to turn yourself in, but no good would come of sparing your life—not for you, nor for anyone else. On the contrary: it would lead only to more bloodshed!'

Shinsuke could not quite grasp what Kinzō was driving at. Had he not owned up to the crimes that weighed on his conscience? And had he not shown penitence for those very same misdeeds? How could he have done this, were he not resolved in his intentions? He failed to see why there should be any cause for worry where his future was concerned. Insisting on his heartfelt sincerity, he repeated his promise, swearing that he would, without fail, hand himself over to the authorities later.

It was as though, having been provoked, the beast in him had been tamed, and Shinsuke once again was rendered the docile, obedient young man that he had formerly been. He recalled the events of that night as though they were a dream in which he had been possessed by a demon. There was even talk of sending him to Ōmiya, in the neighbouring province of Bushū, to wait it out with another gambler, a sworn brother of Kinzō's, but that would have lost him any chance of finding O-Tsuya. Besides, the events of that night had fortunately passed without giving rise to any rumours. The day after the young man's arrival, Kinzō had gone out in the early hours of the morning to take a casual stroll past Lord Hosokawa's mansion; he found there only the trampled remains of what had once been a gift box from the Kawa-chō teahouse, while all traces of blood had been washed away by the rain that night, and even the umbrella, which had been abandoned there, had vanished. As for Seiji, the boatman had apparently assumed that it was Sōta who, after committing the murder, had gone back to steal his money, before killing his wife and going on the run. This being so, even if, by some extraordinary coincidence, he ever happened to come across Shinsuke, there was no need to worry, for, although he would surely be surprised, he would never dream of informing the authorities. All this, Kinzō had learnt from the discreet interrogation of a boatman who was a friend of his. As a next step, he had Shinsuke dispose of his incriminating robes and leant him a winter outfit from his own wardrobe. Lastly, he even went so far as to have Shinsuke apply black marks to his face before sending him out to search every corner of Fukagawa, disguised by day as a pedlar laden with sandals and by night as an itinerant noodle-vendor.

Meanwhile, the old year reached an end and the new one began. Shinsuke had spent every day searching Takabashi, in the neighbourhood of the boatman's house. Less than twenty days had passed since the disappearance of Seiji's wife, but already he had taken a new one, his third, while his business carried on thriving as always. Shinsuke was now convinced that O-Tsuya had already been sold into slavery. Leaving nothing to chance, he returned to Tachibana-chō and furtively peered into the shop where he had once served. Perhaps it was his imagination playing a trick on him, but he saw nothing in the shop, crushed as it was under the leaden weight of silence, to suggest that the young girl had gone home. It was even rumoured in the neighbourhood that the girl's father, racked with anxiety over her fate, had taken seriously ill and been bedridden ever since. Faced thus with the unbearable sorrow that gripped him, Shinsuke understood, deep inside himself, that he would never set foot in Tachibana-chō again.

Abandoning the environs of the Onagi canal for a while, he explored every square inch of places such as Koume, Hashiba and Iriya—areas that were likely home to residences where mistresses were kept—and, needless to say, he searched the other pleasure quarters of the city, too. However, as the second lunar month neared its end, he was still none the wiser as to the girl's whereabouts.

A little later, and the cherry trees came into bloom in Mukōjima, along the banks of the river. A mist rose up towards the tranquil spring sky, and there was a warmth in air that seemed to cast a spell even over Shinsuke as he plied the streets, hawking his wares. With the return of the spring sun, he felt desire, pain and melancholy surge up violently in his breast. He just had to see O-Tsuya once more, if only in his dreams.

It was a beautiful evening towards the end of the third lunar month when Kinzō came home bearing welcome news. 'You know, Shinsuke, this girl you're looking for… I wonder whether she isn't the same one that goes by the name Somekichi, a geisha working in the Naka-chō quarter.'

He said that, having taken a couple of his men to Fukagawa for a drink at the Obana-ya, he had decided on a whim to call for some geisha, and that one of them seemed to be, both in age and looks, the very likeness of the girl for whom Shinsuke had been searching, day in, day out. To begin with, there was the obvious fact of her extraordinary beauty, but there were also her heavy eyelids, her thick, almost masculine eyebrows, her right eye tooth that revealed itself whenever she smiled, adding to her charm, and also the habit she had of biting her lower lip and twisting her mouth a little when engaged in conversation. Finally, there was the erotic charge that she exuded, inflaming men's hearts, with her voice, which was imbued with so much coquetry. These outward signs coincided so exactly with what Kinzō had been told about O-Tsuya that he ventured to make a discreet enquiry about the background of this young woman. During this, he learnt that she was the under the protection of a certain Tokubei, a professional gambler and the boss of the Sunamura gang. He was also able to ferret out that the Tokubei in question was an out-and-out scoundrel, a disreputable sort who was disliked even by those of his own milieu, and that there was, in all likelihood, a friendship between him and the boatman Seiji. With all this material at his disposal, there could scarcely be any doubt. Naturally, Shinsuke was also convinced.

'All in all, it looks like it's her. Only, there's one detail that doesn't fit. I'm afraid you won't thank me for telling you this if she turns out to be the genuine article, but nonetheless…'

Having duly warned Shinsuke, Kinzō reported the rumours circulating about Somekichi. It had been barely a month and a half since she had made her debut in Naka-chō, but she already had a reputation as an accomplished courtesan, intelligent and unrivalled in beauty throughout Fukagawa, where she enjoyed now prodigious popularity. There was talk of an eligible scion of a draper's in Nihonbashi; of an officer from around Kōjimachi—a bannerman of the shogun, no less; and of a good half-dozen other men about town who were flitting about, losing their heads. It was also reported that, despite the exorbitant sums that she extracted from them, she knew how to manipulate each of them so well that none had managed yet to achieve his end. Those in the neighbourhood generally assumed that this Tokubei, being madly in love with her himself, had, for a surfeit of jealousy, prevented her from going further with any of her clients. The madam of the geisha house to which this Somekichi belonged had been none other than Tokubei's mistress, and, although it was with his capital that she had run the business, seemingly not a day had passed when the trio did not clash in never-ending squabbles and fights—the upshot of which was that ten days previously, Tokubei's mistress had been sent packing, and now Somekichi was the most important figure in the house, thus firmly establishing her status as one of the great courtesans of Fukagawa. And so, the gossip was that Tokubei was too heartless a man, of course, but that this Somekichi was possessed of skill well surpassing her years.

However, as if to offer some words of consolation, Kinzō added that it was open to question whether Somekichi really had given herself to Tokubei, as the gossip seemed to make out. 'It's just as likely,' he said, 'that, in chasing after this beauty, Tokubei would be but a toy in her hands. When a woman is the object of so many others' envy, it's inevitable that she should also find herself the object of foolish slander, too. So, if I were you, I shouldn't believe even the half of these rumours.' Nevertheless, given what he had seen in the teahouse, the young woman had conducted herself with a coquettishness so sophisticated that he could scarcely believe she had been brought up in the house of a wealthy pawnbroker until the end of the previous year. He had not seen even the slightest hint of anything to suggest that she was suffering from the loss of a lover. She had laughed gaily throughout the party and had drunk as heartily as few women could. Or had she been trying to drown her sorrows? If she had, she would surely not have lacked good reason for doing so.

'At any rate,' Kinzō concluded, 'tomorrow you shall meet her. I've already left word at the Obana-ya, so you can go and see for yourself.'

The very notion of this Tokubei weighed on Shinsuke's mind, but when he reflected on everything else that he had heard, it all seemed quite plausible. The heavy drinking, the coquettishness, the conspicuous absence of melancholy—all these changes corresponded very well, so he thought, to his image of an O-Tsuya utterly abandoned to debauchery. But then, so long as her feelings for him had not altered, what did it matter what outward signs of depravity she showed?

The following morning, Shinsuke, having shaved the top of his head, bathed and cleaned the black marks off his face, regained the appearance of a clean and presentable young man. Certainly, his soul could not be cleansed of the defilement left by the heinous crimes that he had committed, but his face, now smooth and fresh, was not marked by it in the least and his eyes still shone with that former boyish charm. After Kinzō pointed out to him that if by chance he should come across Seiji, the latter, anxious to cover the traces of his own crimes, could very well set upon him unawares, so they agreed that he should go by palanquin in the early hours of the evening so as not to attract attention. All things considered, the meeting that awaited him with Somekichi would likely mark his farewell to the world.

'Well, I must be going now,' said Shinsuke when the hour arrived at last. 'Thank you for all your help,' he said, his voice filled with deep emotion as he placed his hands to the ground in an expression of gratitude.

'This may very well be the last time we see one another,' replied Kinzō. 'If this Somekichi does turn out to be your O-Tsuya, you needn't trouble yourself to come back here and may go straight to the authorities tomorrow. It will be hard for you, I know, but if you let her keep you for a few days, your resolve will begin to falter. So long as you act like a man and do the honourable thing, you can count on me to take care of the rest. You needn't worry about your father, either.'

Kinzō, in view of Shinsuke's exemplary behaviour ever since he had taken him in, believed that it was fine to send him off like this. Yet he feared that the couple might end their lives in a double suicide at the girl's instigation, and so he asked Shinsuke what he intended to do if indeed he did meet O-Tsuya. Shinsuke assured him without the slightest hesitation that he was firmly resolved to state his case and make her return to her family in Tachibana-chō, satisfying Kinzō, who complimented him on his attitude, happy to have rediscovered the Shinsuke of yesteryear. As a parting gift, he placed in front of Shinsuke an envelope full of money, but since Shinsuke had already put aside all the profits from his hawking in the last four months, he refused Kinzō's generosity, saying that he had no need of it. Kinzō then took back the envelope without ceremony, thinking that it was perhaps better that the young man did not have too much money on him.

That evening, there was a mild breeze blowing gently. It was a veritable spring evening, one in which, shrouded in the gauze of moonlight, the faces of the people in the twilit streets radiated with the pale whiteness of the magnolia flower. The palanquin carrying Shinsuke first sailed along the main avenue in Takabashi, heading straight for Kuroe-chō, then, having swung left at the great torii of the Hachiman shrine, it deposited him in front of the entrance to the Obana-ya. Drinking establishments were not unknown to him, but this was the first time he had set foot inside a teahouse in the red-light district.

Announced as the client sent by the patron from Narihira-chō, Shinsuke was welcomed with all due deference. He was led to the far end of the establishment and shown into a private room, which was lit only by the twinkling lights of the Kurama stone lanterns that dotted the lush vegetation of the garden. He could scarcely believe that amid the rowdy pleasures of the locale there should be a place of such serene elegance.

'I'd like to see the one known as Somekichi,' Shinsuke insisted to the serving girl. 'No other girl will do.'

He might have been taken for a connoisseur who was deliberately behaving like a boor and demanding the most beautiful and famous geisha of all, convinced that he would immediately obtain her favours, so sure was he, in his infatuation, of his incomparable powers of seduction.

Shinsuke idled there, waiting, unsure what to do as he leant against the alcove post. By and by, the low door behind him opened to reveal, under the tiled entrance, the long, slender neck of Somekichi bowed before him. There could no longer be any doubting it, for it was indeed she. Sporting a deliberately light application of white face paint, O-Tsuya had on a large black-satin obi embroidered with gold thread in a design of overlapping chrysanthemums, which was tied about a striped silk-crêpe kimono that revealed beneath it the hem of a robe with a tortoiseshell pattern. Truly, she had been transformed almost beyond recognition, her appearance wholly commensurate with that of the most sought-after geisha in all Tatsumi.

No sooner had she seen the back of the man than she rushed round to see the front, her bare feet thudding across the sticky new tatami mats. With a squeal of recognition, she came crashing down, practically falling into Shinsuke's lap.

'How happy I am to see you safe and sound!' she cried, leaning heavily on his knees as she righted herself. 'You've no idea how I've wanted to see you. Oh, how I've longed to see you!'

To think that it was his fate to give up a woman like this and hand himself in the very next day! When the thought flashed though his mind, Shinsuke suddenly felt a keen attachment to life swell in his breast.

Commencing with O-Tsuya's tale, they began to rake over everything that had gone on since that unforgettable evening in December when they had been separated from

one another. That night, a little after Shinsuke had been
summoned away, the mistress had given the maids and the
young lads the night off, saying that there was nothing more
for them to do and so they could go and amuse themselves.
Left thus alone to watch over the house, O-Tsuya and the
mistress had been chatting together when the ill-famed rain
began falling in sheets. It was just when the downpour was
at its heaviest that Seiji had arrived home, roaring drunk,
with two or three men whom she had never seen before.
Suddenly, without a word, he had had O-Tsuya tied up
and gagged, after which she was bundled into a palanquin
and carried off to Tokubei's house in Sunamura. All this
had clearly been planned in advance, because, in addition
to Tokubei, there were a good half-dozen other cut-throats
lying in wait, keen to have their fun. Having deposited
O-Tsuya in the middle of a spacious room, they had sat in
a circle around her and begun their merrymaking, gulping
down prodigious quantities of alcohol as they teased and
mocked the poor girl. She had understood, though, that she
did not really have to fear for her life. Most of these men
were infatuated with her, and so, if she did not give in to
their advances, they would have little choice but to sell her
elsewhere, and they were hardly going to risk damaging
the 'merchandise'. Counting on this, she made light of
the situation and boldly stood up to the men. Even when

they threatened to kill her, she didn't so much as flinch. Shinsuke's fate was all that she cared about, and this passion had consumed her night and day, robbing her of sleep.

Things turned out just as she had anticipated: shortly thereafter, Seiji had imprisoned her in a locked room, coming daily to woo her.

'I've been so madly in love with you for the longest while,' he would say. 'The thing is, it was I who tricked Shinsuke into eloping with you. But whatever wrong I've done, I did it for you. Won't you consent to be my mistress? If you will, your every wish shall be my command!'

No matter how often she asked what had become of Shinsuke, O-Tsuya could not get a clear-cut answer. Seiji would tell her that it was best to forget all about him, that he had sent him to his father's in Kiyoshima-chō, but she knew that all this was bound to be a lie. By now it was obvious that, though the boatman maintained this pretence, in all the time since he had taken them in, he had never once gone to Tachibana-chō or Kiyoshima-chō. Though O-Tsuya was almost certain that Shinsuke had been murdered, she could not abandon hope so easily.

The term of her imprisonment dragged on terribly, lasting well over two months since that fateful night. All throughout it, Seiji continued visiting her patiently, but for all his threats and entreaties, no matter what he said,

O-Tsuya refused to give in. Tokubei, conscious of what was going on and unable to remain indifferent any longer, took it upon himself to intervene, and at last she was able to leave the room to which she had been confined. Instead, she was placed under strict watch and given domestic chores to do, and was now made the object of their toe-curling flattery. Drastically changing tack, Seiji now endeavoured to buy his way into her affections in so far as was possible.

Tokubei was of a similar age to Seiji, but in terms of villainy, he was a cut above the boatman. He forever maintained an appearance of the utmost calm and never displayed the least anger; he could even give the casual observer the impression of being a benevolent and extremely understanding man. Inserting himself between the two of them, he offered agreeable words to both parties. Behind his friend's back, though, he was especially keen to offer all manner of sympathetic words to O-Tsuya. The young girl immediately suspected that Tokubei had his eye on her, though, and so, feigning receptiveness to this show of sympathy, she worked diligently so that he would lower his guard. Her intention was to flee Sunamura at the earliest opportunity and seek out Shinsuke.

One evening, while plying Tokubei with sake, O-Tsuya said, somewhere between soliloquy and question: 'I've

given up all hope of Shinsuke once and for all now, but I do
wonder whatever has become of him.' Whereupon, to her
surprise, Tokubei's lips hinted at a secret so astonishing that
she had never yet dared to dream it: that, on that fateful
night, Seiji had ordered his faithful Sōta to kill Shinsuke
on the banks of the river; that Sōta had, moreover, taken
it upon himself for whatever reason to strangle his master's
wife and to abscond with her money; and that, afterwards,
Seiji had taken for himself a third wife. None of these
things were said explicitly, of course, but, by piecing everything together, O-Tsuya was able to conclude that this
was more or less the true version of events. In the face of
such evidence, she had little choice but to give up hope of
ever finding Shinsuke again. From that moment, she had
resolved not to let her lover's death go unpunished and
vowed to wreak her vengeance upon Seiji.

It was a little after this that Tokubei had seemingly made
his proposition to the boatman. 'That girl shows no signs
of wavering. And yet, a jewel like that is too precious to be
sold into a brothel. Supposing you were to sell her to me
for a good price? Once she's seen sense, I could set her up
as a geisha through our house in Naka-chō.' At first, Seiji,
who still harboured feelings for the girl in vain, refused in
the strongest possible terms, but, in the end, he relented
and gave up his designs on her.

'You're not exactly unfamiliar with the ways of the world, at any rate. What would really be good is if you were to become a geisha,' said Tokubei so artfully that O-Tsuya could hardly refuse. If she were sent to a brothel, she would inevitably fare far worse. Tokubei had offered to deliver her from that fate, and, in so doing, to keep her virtue intact. Even Shinsuke could not be displeased by such an arrangement, if by chance he got wind of it in the hereafter. And for her part, since she had no intention of ever going back to Tachibana-chō, if she were to make a living on her own, the profession of a geisha was best suited to her temperament. As she mulled it over, it rather seemed to her that she could hardly have hoped for better—and so she consented with surprising ease.

Since her debut as a geisha, O-Tsuya had quickly carved out a first-rate reputation for herself. In a single step, she had managed to pay off her debt and was now in a position to work on her own account. And though she was still financially reliant on Tokubei, at least now she was the mistress of a house. Finding herself thus at liberty to do just as she pleased, she let her thoughts turn once again to Shinsuke. She employed men secretly to find him, but even then her efforts came to naught. Besides, what Tokubei had said about Sōta and Seiji's wife had proved to be true, and so she had little choice but to accept that Shinsuke was, in all likelihood, dead as well. As she resigned herself to fate, one could not say that she was carefree exactly, but it was around this time that her natural vivacity began to re-emerge, and she started living as she saw fit. Truly, there was no occupation more delightful than that of a geisha. What, after all, could be more satisfying than to wheedle money out of fools who let themselves be led on? But now, to crown her happiness, she had been reunited with her former lover, and what an unsurpassed joy it was to know that she could afford to support him from that night forth.

As she related all this to Shinsuke, she imbibed a great deal of sake, and it was with a bleary look, her eyes so bloodshot that you could almost see the blood welling up in them, that she contemplated the young man's face.

'Come, it's been ever so long since you last poured me a drop,' she said, sidling up to him, her cup outheld.

'Forgive me, O-Tsuya. I am no longer worthy of your kindness and favour.'

Brushing away the hand that was drawing near to him, Shinsuke suddenly hastened to adopt a more formal posture and confessed to her the full particulars of his heinous crimes, as though dashing them in the face of this woman whose cup of joy had just overflowed.

'... and that is why tomorrow, I must hand myself over to the authorities. If not, I should be breaking a promise to that gentleman in Narihira. Now that I have seen you, I am prepared to die, so please, forgive me!'

With these words, the man broke down in tears.

'If you must die, then I must die, too... But can you really be so faint-hearted, still?'

O-Tsuya uttered this without any particular display of emotion, slumped there on the floor, as though the alcohol had hewn off her legs, and so slovenly that her words were punctuated by hiccoughs.

'Of course, I was to blame for everything in the beginning,' she continued. 'But the more I hear of your story about killing them, the more I begin to think that you had every reason for doing so. Even where Seiji's wife is concerned, you were only defending yourself, so to speak, so you aren't at all in the wrong. In fact, I'm rather impressed. Come, Shinsuke... Nobody in Narihira is going to report you because you haven't turned yourself in. Besides, nobody else knows about it, and acting in such an absurdly upright way really isn't the done thing any more.'

'I can't believe what I'm hearing!'

He was astounded and fixed her with a look of reproach. But then, once again with tenderness, practically beseeching her, he set about persuading her afresh.

'Of course, it's only natural that you should say this. But all the same, if I were to escape punishment, I should never bear the shame of it. It's only by turning myself over to the authorities, without hiding anything from them, that I'll be able to redeem myself with the master at the Suruga-ya, with the gentleman in Narihira and with my own father in Kiyoshima-chō. In fact, there is something I must ask of you before I depart this world: please, I beseech you, wash your hands of this profession and go back as soon as possible to your parents in Tachibana-chō. Don't you know that your father has been so worried about you that he took to bed last year and has remained there ever since? Compared to the joy that he will feel when he finally sees you again, whatever resentment he may still hold will surely pass. And as for the debts that you owe to Tokubei, I'm certain that he'll settle them as soon as you talk to him.'

'Enough! The thought alone makes me sick!' said O-Tsuya, turning away in displeasure. 'As I already told you, I'd much rather live like this than return to that stuffy old life. So kindly let me be.'

'You're as stubborn-headed as ever! After all I've done, aren't you ashamed that you won't even hear me out when I've come expressly to tell you my last wishes? It's only natural that even the most hardened criminal cannot forget what he owes to his parents. Or has the profession of geisha already corrupted you, body and soul?'

'Yes, it's corrupted me. I am corrupt! I never think about them—not about my father, nor about my mother—never, do you hear me? I don't even see them in my dreams…'

Thus did O-Tsuya reply with affected indifference, but soon enough she collapsed into the man's lap and, sobbing violently, began to plead her case.

'You don't understand anything, Shinsuke, if you quarrel with me like this after being parted for so long. Of course, if these really were your last wishes, I'd listen to you, but there's no way I'm letting you hand yourself over to the authorities. If you mean to die, I simply won't let you! To speak about it in the distant future is one thing, but to do it the day after we meet again is really too heartless of you!'

Wavering before the passion of this woman who remained insensible to both reason and morality, Shinsuke was at a loss for arguments. And yet, though he remained silent, his resolve did not waver. Changing tack, O-Tsuya tried to appeal to his sentiment.

'Well, if there's nothing I can say to change your mind, let us be friends again, at least. And spend a couple of days with me at home, upstairs,' she implored him.

In the struggle between O-Tsuya and his conscience, the former was already winning; however, refusing to admit it to himself, Shinsuke reasoned that, if they were to part over an argument, he would not be able to face death with complete equanimity, and so he resolved, decided to grant her request.

'This isn't the right place to talk all this over. Come, let's go, before you change your mind. We can have a drink at mine…'

Alone rejoicing in this, O-Tsuya staggered to her feet, which had been made weak by all the alcohol, and, taking Shinsuke by the hand, enjoined him to follow her.

Having had the forethought to leave the teahouse separately, the two of them found each other again by the crossroads at Jūniken. The shadows of the two love-birds were projected along the path bathed in the pale shimmer of a mist-veiled moon, and, as they walked, they rediscovered the curious exultation that had taken hold of them when they first ran away together. O-Tsuya occupied a house on an avenue with residences lining only one side, the windows of which overlooked the gardens of the Eitai-ji temple, which stood in the precincts of the Hachiman shrine. Announced by a lantern bearing the name of the establishment—Tsuta-ya—the place was not particularly spacious, but, judging by the arrangement of the living room, on the first floor, with its pillars carved out of carefully selected wood, it seemed well enough designed for her to lead a pleasant existence there with her dresser and two or three apprentice geisha serving under her. Having whispered something in the ear of the young girl who had come to the lattice door at the entrance to greet her mistress, O-Tsuya stepped inside, impatiently removed her geta, and hurriedly led her companion towards the stairs.

Of those moments of joy they had known at the pawn-broker's shop in Tachibana-chō, where their love had been possible only in snatches, hidden from view, and all the sweeter for it; of those dreamlike days, some twenty or so of them, that they had spent at the boatman's house on the banks of the Onagi canal, where they had been subject to the boatmen's gentle teasing—of these, O-Tsuya fondly remembered and, calling to mind their past, lamented the fleeting transience of their love.

'Do you recall those days when you would reproach me for copying the ways of geisha? Well, now you can't have any cause for objection, can you?'

As she spoke, her talk took on all the coarse inflections of a common Fukagawa geisha, and she began to rebuke Shinsuke for his persistence in talking to her like a child. She bid him, if only for that evening, to address her as any true husband would; in return, she too would address him in a more dignified way, as befitted a wife.

Shinsuke, finding that he had already had more than his fill of drink, would have liked to stop, but the young woman, who simply would not listen, kept plying him with sake, practically forcing the liquid past his lips. Experienced drinker though he was, he seemed—perhaps because he had developed a taste for the sake—to hold his drink less well than before, and, as the night progressed, inebriation penetrated him more and more, eventually winning him over.

Having resolved that the next three days would be the last that their love would know, they spent them plunged from dawn till dusk in a kind of whirlwind, chasing down the meals that they had delivered from the Hirasei with countless jugs of sake, each emptied in quick succession, rising and going to bed as the mood took them, so much so, in fact, that, as their last evening approached, such was their exhaustion that, even having sobered, their minds remained in a deep fog.

When Shinsuke looked back on it all, there was not a single joyous memory that he could put his finger on. Indeed, he had been his happiest on that first evening, as they had hurried back from the Obana-ya. That aside, the only thing he remembered, and still only vaguely at that, was the abuse he had hurled at O-Tsuya the following morning, at dawn, suddenly seized by a violent fit of drunkenness.

'You've become quite adept with your tongue, I'm sure,' he had said, 'but I doubt whether deep down in your heart you love me half as much as you used to. That Tokubei is a man of means, and I'm sure he understands many things—there's a world of difference between him and your poor Shinsuke. The sooner I hand myself over to the authorities, the better—for your sake.'

'Oh, drop the act, will you? You needn't play the jealous lover just for my entertainment. It's all too silly to warrant a response. At any rate, I've never yet given myself to any man but you.'

'In that case, Tokubei really has been generous with his money…'

'Am I really so lacking in skill?… I may not have killed a man, Shinsuke, but I've got a far better aptitude for villainy than you.'

Her words instantly satisfied Shinsuke, and, in a voice broken by sobs of great joy, he offered his profuse apologies.

'Forgive me, forgive me,' he repeated himself. 'A wretch like me could never understand anything of a situation like this, so yes, I've had my doubts… but just hearing you say those words means I can now die a happy man.'

'You know,' she said, 'it gladdens me to know that even a man like you, who scarcely ever complains, is capable of these rare moments of jealousy.'

Never had O-Tsuya seemed more lovely to him than she did in that moment. Deep down, he felt so full of courage that now, come what may, he could take anything in his stride.

'Now tell me, Shinsuke,' said O-Tsuya, availing herself of the opportunity to seduce him with words alone, 'what does it matter, three days or four? It's all the same. Come to think of it, why not stay with me three or four months?'

What response was given, Shinsuke could scarcely remember, but what was certain was that he had not said no, that he had shown himself to be quite susceptible to her words and was ready to be led by them. Besides, deep down, that was just what he wanted.

They had then dozed off for a while, and, when they awoke in the early hours of the afternoon, they resumed drinking, but now those intense feelings of pleasure were curiously and wholly absent.

By and by, their last night together arrived, but even as the evening was young, they both sank into a kind of fog. Even had it been despair that led them to drink, the only thing they got out of it, as the drunkenness took hold of them, was a dizzying headache, followed by a heavy melancholy, as the sorrow that follows pleasure came upon on them in successive waves.

After a period of silence, O-Tsuya, who had been lost in thought, suddenly came to herself and began acting like a spoilt child, adopting a studiedly plaintive tone.

'I hope you haven't forgotten what you said to me this morning, Shinsuke?' Even if he would not stay another three or four months, another few days wouldn't hurt, so—and she insisted on this point—why shouldn't they spend another evening in merry drinking before they parted? As for Shinsuke, he continued, as usual, to implore her to return to her parents after he handed himself over the very next day. But since they were both of them so stubborn and strong-willed, and since neither would give an inch, the result was that their paths diverged, and they remained apart as they sank deeper and deeper into misery.

'Oh, what's the use? What's the use of it all?!' O-Tsuya said disconsolately, getting to her feet. Eventually, she returned with her shamisen and threw open the shoji leading onto the veranda. There, perching on the ledge, she struck up some measures of a katō-bushi melody. The warbling sensuousness of that voice in which she took so much pride spread through the room, drifting out into the street, where several passers-by stopped to listen. 'Can you really not grasp the meaning of this ballad? Can you really still mean to leave me after hearing my song?' she would ask now and then as she glanced at him from the corner of her eye, her gaze full of bitterness. Outside, beyond the balustrade on the veranda, a beautiful starlit nightscape stretched out above the trees of the Eitai-ji temple, as though peering down at the figure of the young woman.

Just then, there was the sound of footsteps coming up the stairs, and the sliding screen shot open.

'Shinsuke, I presume? Allow me to introduce myself. Tokubei, of Sunamura.'

Standing at the threshold, the man bowed his head with deep respect, a handsome leathern tobacco pouch dangling from his right hand. Dressed in a padded silk kimono with a fine mesh pattern, over which he had draped a hanten of dappled indigo, he was a man of prosperous dimensions, smooth of manner and so too, apparently, of mind.

'Can't I have a moment's peace? I'm right in the middle of practising!'

Her admonishment was thrown at the two men brusquely, just as they were about to exchange the customary greetings. But, without so much as glancing in their direction, she played on.

'I'm sorry to disturb you,' said Tokubei, turning to O-Tsuya, 'but there is an urgent matter that I must discuss with you. Might I have a word with you downstairs? I shan't keep you long.'

In this moment, his eyes sought hers with a strange gleam, intent on conveying some kind of message.

'I know what it is that you want me for, but not for anything will I be prised away from here tonight. You can't possibly think that I'll go anywhere, leaving behind the love of my life.'

'That's where you're wrong, because it just so happens that it's Shinsuke here that I've come to talk to you about.'

'How long exactly have you been here, anyhow?' asked O-Tsuya, at last setting aside her shamisen. 'It's most odd that you should recognize Shinsuke without ever having met him.'

'I've only just arrived, as it happens. But I heard you from downstairs. "Shinsuke! Shinsuke!" you kept calling. So it must be him, I thought to myself. Anyhow, Shinsuke,' he said, turning to the young man, 'you've given O-Tsuya quite the greatest happiness by turning up safe and sound like this, when everyone else thought you were dead.'

'That's why I've asked you not to disturb us,' O-Tsuya continued. 'If you have something to say, then say it here.'

'Aha!... How's that now? Now that you've found him again, you've all the time in the world for your sweet nothings. It won't take long. Just a moment of your time downstairs, if you please.'

Seized by an inexplicable sense of anguish, Shinsuke watched on in silence as they bandied words. At first, he could not help worrying where their talk might lead—but seeing how Tokubei held his composure put his mind at ease, and he even ended up sympathizing with him on account of O-Tsuya's capricious obstinacy. In his candour, Shinsuke was astonished to see how she treated 'the Boss of Sunamura' like a mere plaything, and, deep down within himself, he marvelled yet again that his O-Tsuya of yesteryear had become this impressive Somekichi.

'Now, now, O-Tsuya…' he whispered, in a voice that was as low as it was hesitant. 'You really mustn't talk like that when the boss has taken the trouble to come here. Seeing as we're not exactly busy right now, you should be a good girl and do as he asks.'

'If you say so…'

As she acquiesced—miracle that it was—her face instantly broke into a sardonic grin. Having fixed a few stray hairs in front of the mirror, she adjusted the collar of her haori and turned to him, saying: 'While I'm gone, be a good boy, won't you? I wouldn't have gone for anything else, but seeing as it's about you, I can't very well rest without knowing what it is.'

'Oh, it's nothing to trouble yourself over. In your own time, O-Tsuya…'

With this, she and Tokubei went downstairs.

Could it be that someone had come from Narihira to take him back? Or that the boatman Seiji had got wind of his presence there and had enjoined Tokubei to stage an intervention? Despite his words of reassurance, Shinsuke could not but feel worried. In the latter scenario, he hadn't much to fear, as he would hand himself in the very next day, but the first was a different matter altogether: how, then, could he justify himself to Kinzō? Had he not clearly broken the promise that he had made as he left Narihira— to go without fail and hand himself over to the authorities?

'O-Tsuya is a remarkable woman, to be sure! But how is it that, as soon as I find myself together with her, I lose all my resolve? No matter what, I must surrender myself tomorrow morning!'

Talking to himself in this way, Shinsuke tried to muster his courage.

Downstairs, the conversation seemed to drag on. From time to time, he could hear a pipe being tapped, but not the slightest burst of O-Tsuya's voice, ordinarily so high-pitched, reached the upper floor. A good hour or so seemed to go by before he finally heard a woman's voice declaim: 'Wait here a minute while I go and see what he says.' Then O-Tsuya came hurrying up the stairs, and, with an air of grave concern, she rushed over to Shinsuke, half crouching, bringing her face close to his.

'Whatever's the matter?' he asked, no longer able to hold back when he saw the look on her face.

'Shinsuke, I don't suppose…' she began, but suddenly, checking herself, she got to her feet again and went over to the top of the stairs to make sure that nobody was eavesdropping there or behind the sliding screen. Having satisfied herself, she returned to Shinsuke and continued: 'I don't suppose you'd mind if I told Tokubei about what you've done and how you intend to hand yourself over to the authorities tomorrow?… Would you?… Even if you would, I'm afraid it's too late now. The fact is, I've taken the initiative and told him everything…'

Shinsuke blanched. Though he had made up his mind, he would have preferred to rank among the virtuous during what little time he had left in the world.

'In a sense, it really doesn't matter. But since it's not exactly the sort of thing one tells people, I'd much rather have kept it quiet.'

'But, Shinsuke, if I hadn't told him, your life would have been in danger…'

After casting another worried look at the sliding screen, she continued:

'What Tokubei wanted to tell me was that, since it was you, Shinsuke, the man I love, you could stay here for as long as you wanted and that it didn't bother him in the least. But in return, he wants to borrow me tonight. You see, he needs me to go with him to Mukōjima, to the villa of a high-ranking vassal of the shogun, a certain Serizawa, from whom he expects to make a lot of money by using me as bait. I pleaded with him again and again to put it off, saying that I couldn't, since I'd be so worried about leaving you here. Then again, if it weren't for you, I would be going to Mukōjima this evening. I did promise, after all, but now something about it doesn't seem quite right… You know, for all his fine words, what Tokubei really wants is to tie me down with money someday and have his way with me. So I wondered whether he might not use my absence somehow to lure you away and kill you. Or it even occurred to me that Seiji might have found you and asked Tokubei to kill you. That's why I thought that if he only knew that you were intending to turn yourself over to the authorities tomorrow, he would give up whatever it is he's planning. So, I told him the whole story. What choice did I have?'

'What did he say, then?'

'He was stunned to learn that such a delicate-looking man as you had killed. But it's all right. It gave him such a fright that he isn't going to do anything rash. So much for that. But, you see, Shinsuke, from what he's said, I really don't see how I can get out of this tonight. I'll have to set off for Mukōjima shortly…'

Since she would not return until the following morning, O-Tsuya then insisted that Shinsuke stay another night.

She said that if it were any ordinary client, she would of course break off the meeting, but to refuse going to Serizawa's villa in Mukōjima that evening would be a great mistake—the money alone was in the order of one hundred ryo. If that weren't enough, the reality was, she claimed, that this was all part of an elaborate scheme of blackmail and deceit that she had hatched with Tokubei in order to extort a large sum of money, and so putting it off even by a few hours could jeopardize the whole plan... Thus, using this as a pretext and adding all manner of exaggeration, did she plot to keep Shinsuke by her side a while longer.

The more Shinsuke heard, the more he was appalled by her depravity. That a woman, who only yesterday had been the young mistress of the Suruga-ya household, was now conspiring to blackmail a vassal of the shogun, and who knew what else besides... He was aghast at the very thought of it. How could such a change have taken place? No longer did he have the courage to remonstrate with her: his only thought was to escape this peril as quickly as possible.

'Certainly, you cannot refuse such an important occasion. As for my part, I've nothing further to say, and my staying here, for however long, won't change anything, so let's turn these circumstances to our advantage and part ways now. Sooner? Later? What does it matter when I hand myself in?'

Her head downcast, buried in thought, O-Tsuya gloomily prodded at the ashes in the brazier until at last, as though having come to a decision, she lifted her head and said with absolute clarity:

'Well, if your mind is made up, so be it. It's too late anyhow. To tell you the truth, I was hoping to keep you another day and win you over somehow, but now I've given up all hope of that. When I said I was going to Mukōjima, that much was true, but I lied when I said I'd be returning tomorrow. I'll be back in the small hours of the morning. Wait for me, won't you? I'll come, I promise.'

Shinsuke had barely agreed to this when the girl, seized apparently by yet greater fears, declared that she would rather he came to fetch her around the midnight hour disguised as her hakoya—which is to say, her shamisen-carrier. When Shinsuke refused this idea out of hand, O-Tsuya flew into a rage. How dare he deny her this last wish? She wouldn't let the matter go, however, saying that if he refused, there would be no question of her going, no matter what Tokubei said or did. In the end, Tokubei intervened, and, no matter how he tried to appease or coax her, O-Tsuya remained implacable. Only with great difficulty did he manage to prevail at last upon Shinsuke.

4

A T THE TOLLING of the midnight hour, some three
hours or so after O-Tsuya and Tokubei had departed,
Shinsuke headed out to fetch them, disguised as a shamisen-
carrier. To reach this villa at Mukōjima, which was situated
a few hundred yards past the sanctuary at Akiba, right in
the middle of the rice fields at Terajima-mura, he carefully
followed the directions that had been given him. Since his
destination lay a good few miles from Naka-chō, he had
been advised to travel part of the journey by palanquin;
however, he wanted to absorb, as he went, the spectacle of
Edo's nightscape, thus imprinting on his mind the imagery
of this world that he was about to depart.

As soon as he set foot beyond the pleasure district,
he found not a single house still awake, nor a single
person in the deserted streets. Having been corrupted,
body and soul, by the orgy of his three-day sojourn
on the upper floor of the Tsuta-ya, Shinsuke now took
pleasure in the rejuvenating sense of solitude and the
cool night breeze.

As he crossed the Azuma bridge, he suddenly recollected the people in Kiyoshima-chō and Narihira. Turning towards each of them in turn, he placed his hands together and prayed from the bottom of his heart that his father and Kinzō should forgive him, for the next morning he would do the honourable thing. Having crossed the Makura bridge, he found himself walking along the embankment under a splendid canopy of cherry blossoms; a waning moon of copper hue hung high overhead, its reflection on the water's face seeming to forebode some evil that it alone knew. He paused there awhile, gazing at the luminous sky and the black waves that lapped imperturbably. Now and then, pleasure boats carrying belated fares to Yoshiwara passed by in ones and twos, gliding stealthily up the deserted watercourse in the direction of the San'ya canal.

What wicked deeds could O-Tsuya have planned that night with Tokubei? 'So young, and yet so bold!'—Kinzō's words in relating Somekichi's ill repute throughout Naka-chō appeared to have been well justified. In his remorse, Shinsuke had once believed that, were it not for his crimes, he could have made a life with this woman, but if she was indeed the shameless creature that rumour held her to be, then, he told himself, even if he had remained blameless, they could never have married. Reasoning thus, he found it easier to resign himself to his fate… As he turned all this over and over in his mind, he made his way down the slope at Ushi-no-Gozen.

The villa at Terajima-mura was easily found. Shinsuke was aware, of course, that it was the residence of a high-ranking samurai—a bannerman, no less—but still, he could not but be impressed, despite the darkness shrouding the place, by the grandeur and opulence of this imposing edifice, enclosed as it was by a hedgerow grown directly behind a wall of closely knotted bamboo laths in the style of the Kennin-ji temple. Casting an inquisitive glance through a gap in the gate at the rear of the property, he saw that, in spite of the late hour, the kitchen shutters had been left slightly ajar. But if he could make out the faint glow of lamplight coming from within, the sound of voices was curiously absent.

'Good evening!' he announced himself, venturing through the gate, which he found unbolted. 'I'm sorry to bother you. I'm from the call office in Naka-chō…'

'From the call office? Whatever are you doing here at this hour?'

Through the half-open kitchen shutters, a man, probably an attendant, poked his head out and, in the light of the lantern that came with it, eyed Shinsuke warily.

'Well…' Shinsuke gave an embarrassed laugh. 'Well, you see… It's just that I've come to fetch Miss Somekichi, and—'

'What?' the attendant thundered before Shinsuke had time to finish speaking. 'To fetch Miss Somekichi? I see… We've got a joker, have we? I dare say you must be part of that gang as well. Well, you're too late. We've got your number. If you really think that you can cheat His Lordship and extort a pretty penny out of him, then I'm afraid you're mistaken!…'

Dumbfounded by this, Shinsuke was still at a loss for words when suddenly shouts and cries began to issue from one of the back rooms.

'What? A scam?!… Don't play the fool with me! You wanted the girl and gave her the money, and now you've the front to call it a scam?!…'

These fiery words were undoubtedly Tokubei's.

Then, much like the calm before a storm, a spell of stillness descended over the room. It was broken only by the clear and audacious voice of O-Tsuya, who was still in perfect control of herself.

'Since the game's up, there's no point in hiding it any longer,' she said. 'So what if Tokubei and I did arrange a little trap for you? Don't you think that in your position, it would be better to resign yourself to having been swindled like a fool and to draw a line under it? Otherwise, if you're so very deeply outraged, then don't be shy: why not pull out your sabre or pike and kill us both?! But let me tell you: a hundred ryo or a thousand ryo, you won't see *any* of it again.'

'You bastard!' Tokubei suddenly cried out. 'Who are you to draw your sword at me?!'

'This one's only a third-rate swordsman. He's just trying his luck,' O-Tsuya drawled in a shrill voice, carrying above the din of the violent clash that had now erupted in the room.

Feet smashing against screens, bodies crashing down upon the tatami mats, the ringing and clattering of swords—then, just as Shinsuke heard a long howl of pain, Tokubei ran out, his round face bloodied as he made a dash for the kitchen door. Her hair in disarray, O-Tsuya followed hot on his heels, only to be stopped by Serizawa, who grabbed her by the collar of her kimono and forced her to the ground, while with his other hand he raised his sword overhead, threatening her.

Without a word, Shinsuke leapt over from the kitchen and clung to the samurai's wrist.

'My Lord, it's only too understandable that you're angry, but, please, the girl isn't to blame. Show some mercy, I beseech you!'

'Who are you?' Serizawa asked, as he turned to look, lowering his weapon.

He was a fine-looking man of around thirty-five, with handsome features and a delicately bluish skull where the razor had passed; a man who, in his silk kimono the colour of smoked bamboo with its black velvet obi tied around it, had an air of elegance and refinement.

'I, sir? Why, I am a humble shamisen-carrier, sent here from Naka-chō to fetch Miss Somekichi. I do not pretend to know what has come to pass here, but for a man of your station, such recklessness could only leave you open to scandal. Please, I beg of you, put away your sword.'

'This night, you shall be spared,' said Serizawa, letting go of the woman brusquely. 'As for the money, you can keep it. Call it a severance fee, and never let me see you here again.'

With these words, he swept off into the inner rooms of the villa.

'See me here again?!' cried O-Tsuya after him, cursing. 'I'd never come back even if you begged me.'

The attendant who had greeted Shinsuke must have gone off somewhere, for he was nowhere to be seen. Only Tokubei remained, sitting on the kitchen step, groaning in pain as he cradled his slashed face in his hands. In addition to his head, he had sustained severe cuts to his arms and thighs, and the poor fellow writhing there, half dead and half alive, was a mere shadow of the robust man that Shinsuke had encountered only that afternoon.

'O-Tsuya! O-Tsuya!' he cried out in a feeble, breathless voice. 'His blows hit none of my vital organs, but with all the blood I'm losing, I know that I'm done for... That bastard Serizawa!... You must get Shinsuke to help you... and kill that son of a bitch!... You must avenge me!'

'Oh, give it a rest, won't you?... Why, he barely scratched you! It's beneath you to make such a fuss about nothing. But I've a feeling that wretched attendant's gone to raise the alarm. There's no time to lose. Take my arm and let's go before he comes back with the police.'

Taking him unceremoniously by the arm, O-Tsuya hauled Tokubei to his feet.

The very mention of the police sent Shinsuke into a panic. If he were arrested in the villa, how would he manage to explain away his presence there while a crime was being perpetrated? Yet he could not think of abandoning the two of them to their fate, and so, in the end, he found himself, somewhat reluctantly, assisting O-Tsuya. Having both passed an arm under Tokubei's shoulders, they hurried off, dragging him along in their flight.

Taking the back lane that ran between the rice fields and passed by few other residences, the three of them dashed in a mad frenzy for five or six chō, before finally taking shelter in the shadows of a tree-lined alley and catching their breath as best they could. Fortunately, no police detachment seemed to show up. Shinsuke tore the towel that he had been carrying into strips and began to dress

Tokubei's wounds, which were still bleeding heavily. They were all three of them covered in so much blood that it was impossible to tell which of them was in fact injured.

'I've become a real burden to you, Shinsuke!' said Tokubei plaintively, resting in the girl's lap as she sat by the roadside. 'I'll be fine if I can just make it home... I owe you my life.'

'Are you sure you'll be all right? Do you think you can manage to walk?' O-Tsuya enquired after a moment's rest, sweetly and with seemingly genuine concern. 'If not, we'll carry you between us. Just try to stand up and see how you go.'

'I'm fine now, don't you worry!' he answered, struggling to his feet, only to stumble and have to cling to the girl's arm once again.

'Now look here, you're in no fit state to walk. Wouldn't it be better...'

Grabbing the staggering man suddenly by the hair, she threw him to the ground with a violent thud.

'... if you just died right here!'

Before he knew it, O-Tsuya had extracted a razor that she had hidden in the folds of her obi and was brandishing it under his nose. Tokubei had just enough time to grab her wrist from below and, with the strength that comes in the face of certain death, push her off, trying to slash at her in turn with a fish knife, shouting all the while: 'If I'm to die, then I'm taking you with me!'

The suddenness of the thing had taken Shinsuke completely off guard. In the blinding darkness, he could not distinguish clearly what was going on, and so he began to circle around the two adversaries. When he finally spotted Tokubei entangled in the girl's legs, he dived into the fray and, grabbing him by the scruff of the neck, dragged him out.

'In on it and intent on killing me as well, I suppose? Well, let's be having you then!' said the wounded man, who now, in a burst of desperate energy, set upon Shinsuke.

The young man quickly wrested the weapon out of his hand, while at the same time O-Tsuya stood up and tripped Tokubei, sending him crashing to the ground, where a fierce struggle once again ensued. Despite Tokubei's injuries, however, O-Tsuya was no match for the man's brute strength, and she eventually found herself on her back, pinned to the ground, her throat constricted by fingers determined to choke the very life out of her. Had the wounded man had even an ounce of strength left, her fate would have been quickly sealed, but Tokubei was already too weak for that.

'What are you just standing there for, Shinsuke?!' O-Tsuya cried out for help in a half-strangled voice. 'He's trying to kill me, the bastard!... Tonight is our chance to do away with him... Don't you see? We'll be free!... There won't be another chance like it!... I'm begging you, Shinsuke, hurry up and...'

As she begged him, her life seemed to be hanging by a thread, her voice fading and fading until it seemed on the brink of being silenced once and for all.

'I can't hold on much longer, damn it!... Do something, Shinsuke!'

Once again, she let out a shriek. At that very moment, just as her voice was about to give out, Shinsuke plunged the blade of the knife that he had seized into the back of the wounded man straddling her body. This was not enough to stop him, however, and, grappling and struggling violently with Shinsuke, Tokubei kicked, punched, bit and clawed at him. Neither during Sōta's murder, nor during that of the boatman's wife, had Shinsuke encountered such savage resistance. The two men fought on: sometimes on their feet, sometimes on the ground, where they rolled, crawled on all fours and grabbed each other by the hair. At last, almost by chance, Shinsuke managed to land a blow right on his opponent's side.

'He... Hey! O-Tsuya!... I may be about to die, but my spirit will come back to haunt you, mark my words!'

With this curse on his lips, Tokubei gave a convulsive shudder as a second blow was sent through his heart.

One sharp cry of agony, and he stiffened in the arms of his rival.

'I'd like to see you try…' said O-Tsuya.

'A third one! I'm done for, O-Tsuya!' said Shinsuke, freeing himself from the dead man's clutch and shoving the corpse aside. 'Come and die together with me, I implore you!'

His teeth were chattering in terror.

'What talk! If that was your plan, then what was the sense in killing him? You've gone this far, after all. All we have to do is play innocent, and nobody will be any the wiser. You must try to take it all in your stride. I, for one, have no intentions of dying, thank you very much.'

Shinsuke was no longer capable of reason. That he had played right into her hand was obvious; and yet now, at last, he relinquished the resolve to which he had so stubbornly clung these past three days.

'So, you agree? Ah, how happy that makes me!' O-Tsuya cried, dancing wildly for joy and throwing herself into the arms of her blood-smeared lover.

Shinsuke, however, was sunk in thought, dead to the world around him. So, leaving him to one side, O-Tsuya set about disposing of the body herself. 'You won't be needing this where you're going,' she said, slipping her hand under Tokubei's kimono and extracting the money belt containing the hundred ryo. Then, undressing the corpse completely, she gathered all his clothes into a small pile and tied them up with a length of string, intending to dispose of the incriminating items. To complete her work, she took out her razor and began to slash Tokubei's face in all directions, before submerging him under the mud of the rice field. Thus, even if the corpse were to be discovered, they would not have to fear his identification.

Later that evening, taking the less frequented paths, they picked their way stealthily back to Naka-chō.

5

IN THE AFTERMATH, Tokubei's henchmen in Sunamura conducted a thorough search for him, but their efforts came to naught. Lord Serizawa did admit, under questioning, to having given him a good few blows of his sabre, but he said that Tokubei had fled the scene with his two accomplices. As for O-Tsuya, her account held that the three of them had lost each other as they made their escape, fearing the arrival of the police, and that she had not seen him since. Even if he had managed to get away, she opined, there was very little chance of his being alive after sustaining such wounds.

With little short of the devil's own luck, the couple had, for the moment, pulled the wool over the eyes of the world. Fearing nobody, they plunged themselves now into a life of gaiety and laughter. Though subject to malicious rumour, Somekichi's reputation continued to grow in Naka-chō, and her golden age seemed destined to last for ever. One fine morning, however, a fortnight after the night of the crime, a figure appeared unexpectedly at the entrance to the Tsuta-ya: it was none other than Kinzō, and he was demanding to be received. Shinsuke, who at the time lay slumped by the brazier, sipping his morning sake, was astonished to hear his voice and immediately ran upstairs.

Meanwhile, down below, O-Tsuya and Kinzō began to remonstrate.

'But I'm telling you that I don't know the man!' she said brusquely, feigning ignorance to the very last.

'If you say he isn't here, then I won't waste your time or mine. It isn't worth having the house searched, because until the man concerned is ready to play the game, nothing will come of it. So, I'll go home. But if you ever happen to come across this man, don't forget to tell him from me: tell him that even if his word means nothing, I am a man who keeps my promises. So, he can rest assured. No indiscretion will ever pass my lips. But, seeing that life is so dear to him now, he had better mend his ways—start from scratch and in future adopt an attitude that doesn't put me to shame or him in any more danger. Since he left my house, he cannot have done much good, but at least, from now on, he can turn his back on the path that he's been following. You won't forget to tell him, will you, dear lady? And pray do forgive the intrusion.'

With these words, he took his leave.

JUN'ICHIRŌ TANIZAKI

'Well, that wasn't so hard, was it?' said O-Tsuya, looking very pleased with her performance as she climbed the stairs. Finding Shinsuke there in the depths of melancholy, she made an audacious suggestion. 'If you're so worried about it, why not do away with him as well?'

'I'd thought of that myself,' he replied, 'but to kill him—him of all people—would incur the wrath of heaven, I suspect.'

In fact, things had reached the stage whereby his mind seemed to be filled constantly with plots of murder and theft. For this couple, whose union had been forged in the heat of such bloody misdeeds, any pleasure not enlivened by the piquancy of murder, in the end, seemed very bland indeed. Shinsuke had only to look at a face, and he would imagine at once a scene in which that person would become but a gruesome corpse. All told, it seemed inevitable that others yet would meet a brutal end at his hands.

It was around that time that business brought the boatman Seiji back into O-Tsuya's life. With his trade flourishing, and what with all manner of illicit incomes to compound this, he prospered all year round and had lately had his house rebuilt in great style. In the world of Takabashi, he now ranked among the established men of fortune. Having won the respect of his fellow boatmen, and with little to fear now that Tokubei was, to all appearances, dead, he returned to past regrets and lingering affections and, putting his best foot forward, sought once again to melt O-Tsuya's heart.

Harbouring some ulterior motive from the outset, O-Tsuya treated him with deliberate indulgence and, manipulating him with great skill, plotted to cheat him out of some considerable money before tossing him aside.

'If you really do think about me so much,' she said, 'I can hardly blame you, but since you have your O-Ichi now, it somehow doesn't feel quite right...'

Thus would she always escape his advances with an evasive response. The O-Ichi in question was none other than Seiji's third wife, a former geisha from Yoshi-chō, whom he had made his mistress some two or three years prior, and whom he had installed in his house shortly after his wife's murder. She was far from being a great beauty, yet she had, for some reason or other, an unaccountably strong hold over the man. Infidelities on his part, or even the slightest misdemeanour, if discovered, were sure to result in a connubial tirade, during which she was wont to grab him by the collar and box his ears. And however much he longed for O-Tsuya, the one thing he could apparently never manage was to get rid of O-Ichi.

'But what does she matter?' he would say. 'There are any number of ways to arrange it without her knowing.'

'No, I cannot agree to that. If you really do love me, then just get rid of her and make me your wife,' O-Tsuya would counter-propose, putting Seiji in a most awkward position.

However, one day, having carefully chosen the hour, she suggested something else entirely. 'Now, Seiji… You say you love me, but the truth is that these are just words. If you love me truly, wouldn't the best thing be to do away with her good and proper, since she's wise to all your less reputable dealings? After all, you killed Shinsuke for less, so you can't say you don't have it in you…'

'That was Sōta!' he retorted, taken aback by this. 'I had no part in it!… My, you've become a real piece of work lately, haven't you?'

For all his astonishment, Seiji seemed to be rather taken with O-Tsuya's bold suggestion.

Later, as they lay whispering sweet nothings in the privacy of their own bed on the top floor of the Tsuta-ya, O-Tsuya would turn to her lover and say: 'Soon you'll see, Shinsuke… A little more time, and we'll have our revenge on Seiji and his wife.'

As they waited for the right moment, savouring the prospect of it, Shinsuke was continually on his guard, and, whenever he went out, morning or night, he would try in as far as was possible not to let anybody see his face.

The opportunity finally came in the seventh lunar month of the year. After the arrest of one of Seiji's men, the extent of his crimes gradually came to light, and soon enough he found it necessary to vacate his house and flee for a while to the countryside. Intending to take advantage of the circumstances to get rid of the of the cumbersome O-Ichi, he desired O-Tsuya to abscond with him and suggested spiriting her away secretly by boat, under cover of night, of course taking with them all the money that was to hand. No sooner had his words reached O-Tsuya's ears than, suppressing the palpitations of her heart, she gave her immediate consent.

It was decided that O-Ichi would at last be dispatched just before midnight on the fourth or fifth evening after O-Bon, after which they would vacate the capital. By then, Seiji was to have completed all his careful preparations, let go the many staff that he employed, sold off household items and furniture, and have only his wife with him, who would be told that she alone would accompany him on the escape. He sent a message to O-Tsuya, informing her that on the strike of the fourth hour of the evening, she was to steal through the back door, by which time O-Ichi's fate would be sealed.

Having arranged everything with Shinsuke in advance, O-Tsuya arrived at the boatman's house alone, her face hidden by a long veil, and, at the agreed hour, she entered the premises through the kitchen door.

'This way! This way!' Seiji called out from the large tatami room at the rear, where, by the light of a lantern, he stood proudly, like a guardian deity at a temple. At his feet, bent backwards and arms outstretched, lay the body of O-Ichi.

'I've just finished it... She really put up a fight!' he said, still trying to catch his breath.

'What does she look like? Let me see.'

With perfect composure, O-Tsuya pulled up the wick of the lantern and peered down at the victim. Perhaps because of the blood that had been sent to her head during the strangulation, O-Ichi's complexion looked beautifully fresh, as though she were still alive. The expression of agony that lingered on her features looked more like a grin, and it was only her glaring pupils, trained on the ceiling, that betrayed something more terrifying.

'The boat's ready and waiting just outside. We'll load her on to it, and if we throw her overboard once we're in open water, she should sink to the bottom... This is all the money I could get...'

With a dull thud, Seiji set down before O-Tsuya a heavy-looking jute sack, which must have contained about five hundred ryo in smaller denominations.

It was then that the back door once again slid open quietly, as none other than Shinsuke stole into the house.

'It's been quite a while, Seiji. I really must thank you for all that you've been doing for O-Tsuya...'

'What?! You, Shinsuke...' said Seiji, turning deathly pale.

The figure standing before him and blocking his way had just untied the kerchief with which he had been concealing his face, and the more Seiji looked at him, the more certain he grew that this man, with his luxuriant locks, in his gaily coloured blue-and-white tie-dyed yukata and a candy-striped waistband, was indeed none other than Shinsuke.

'The very same, and yet altogether a different man than the one you knew. For it was I who killed your wife and that bastard Sōta. Yes, it was all my handiwork.'

A scuffle ensued after a brief exchange of words, but since Seiji had no weapon to hand, he was soon enough struck by his opponent's blade. He wanted to cry out for help, but O-Tsuya leapt up behind him and prevented him, stopping his mouth firmly with her hand, while Shinsuke finished the job.

The bag of five hundred ryo that they had stolen from Seiji was lavished on their orgies of luxury and reckless

139

abandon, and, by the close of that same year, it had been spent in its entirety. For indeed, the love of this monstrous couple had now endured, to be exact, one whole year.

'I hope something nice comes our way soon, otherwise it won't be much of a New Year, will it?' they would often whisper to one another, lamenting their reduced means. But in the absence of any easy fortune, the burden of support fell to O-Tsuya, who drew on every last one of her talents so that she might swindle her clients as best she could.

As he sank deeper into debauchery, Shinsuke's amorous feelings for O-Tsuya turned into an all-consuming passion, and whenever she would come home late at night with the explanation that she had been 'at work', he was wont to pour such terrific scorn on her.

'You really are impossible, you know,' she would always reply with a laugh, as though dismissing him out of hand. 'These are the lengths I go to because of my love for you, and this is how you repay me! Anyway, if I were having an affair, I daresay you'd know about it… How do you expect me to work like this?'

If the late nights were not enough, there were even times when O-Tsuya would not come back until the following morning, giving Shinsuke a sleepless night as he waited for her. Whenever he would reproach her, filled as he was with misgiving, she would invariably brush it off, insisting on her chastity and replying that there was far more to the art of a geisha than met the eye, that, if you really wanted to work a client, you were forever having to feign inebriation and carry on like that throughout the night, and that if you didn't have the knack for it, you would wind up empty-handed. For all his wrongs, Shinsuke was a straightforward man at heart and had kept this world entirely at arm's length. And since Somekichi—his own O-Tsuya—was the only geisha he knew, he would experience periods of intense jealousy, but always end up believing her.

O-Tsuya, however, seemed to be sleeping elsewhere more and more frequently these days. Whenever she came back, she would take pains to enumerate at great length the names of all the clients and venues to which she had been summoned the previous night, yet she forever seemed ill at ease now, and her cool demeanour had vanished entirely. A suspicious mind might have wondered whether she was not in the grip of a happiness that was just too much for her to hide.

One evening, she came back roaring drunk, clinging to the arm of a client who had seen her home.

'Shinsuke!' she called out with a tongue tinged with venom. 'Here is the man who has lately become my danna, my most esteemed patron. Since he isn't entirely unknown to you, why don't you come and make peace with him? And don't forget your manners…'

Her *danna* was none other than the man with whom she and Tokubei had come to such terrible blows: Lord Serizawa.

Shinsuke had caught only a glimpse of him that night, but now that he could see the man up close, his previous impression was confirmed: yes, indeed, with his noble mien and handsome features, he cut an imposing figure, and the dignity of his rank commanded natural respect.

Ah, so it is him, Shinsuke said to himself, having almost intuited it.

'Shinsuke, I presume?… It's all water under the bridge, my boy. I should like for us to be reconciled. We'd be delighted if you'd come and stay at the villa in Terajima-mura sometime.'

As he spoke, a smile passed over Serizawa's thin, knowing lips. He seemed to be prodigiously drunk.

Finding himself suddenly in the grip of burning jealousy, Shinsuke remained silent, waiting to get his hands on solid evidence. He knew from experience that if he said anything rash, he risked O-Tsuya turning the tables on him, and so he decided to try manoeuvring her into an impossible position. Thus, every evening he would make discreet enquiries to find out where she was going; he won the trust of other geisha and had them report back all the rumours about her clients. Finally, after a good month of investigating, he was satisfied that what he had imagined more or less corresponded to the truth. What he had managed to find out provided only circumstantial evidence, however, for no matter how he tried, he was never able to catch them in the act. O-Tsuya, so sure of herself and of Shinsuke's docile mind, would never fail, on her return, to spout off, in a sincere tone, a whole tissue of shameless lies about customers scattered at the four cardinal points, when in fact she had not once left the mansion of Lord Serizawa. Having divined her duplicitous conduct, Shinsuke found it increasingly difficult to contain his rage, and, on the evening of the third day of the New Year, he subjected her to a ruthless interrogation.

'Well, when you put it that way, what can I say? Evidently, you're no longer quite as naïve as you once were…'

If Shinsuke had expected outright denial, what he got was an icy look and stinging scorn.

'… You aren't at all mistaken that I'm selling my favours to Serizawa. But really, Shinsuke, try to think about it rationally… What do you expect if you mean to court a geisha? Even a woman of my talents can't expect to pay her bills by conversation alone… Surely you ought to have worked that out for yourself by now? After all, I'm not doing any of this for fun. It's to keep you in clover that I'm going to such arduous lengths. You should be grateful rather than making lewd innuendos... If I were you, I'd keep my ears and mouth shut. But since we're at it, I may as well enlighten you: there were times when I gave myself to Seiji, and to Tokubei as well. To have gone so long without realizing it is hardly to your credit.'

Taunted and abused, Shinsuke flew into a sudden rage. O-Tsuya's real intention, in throwing oil on the fire like this, seemed to be to drive a wedge between them—one that would put an end to the relationship once and for all.

'What a fool I've been! Never would I have suspected you of such callousness. How could you deceive me like this?!'

Suddenly, he took her by the collar of her kimono, threw her to the ground and, having seized a handy bamboo hanger, set about beating her mercilessly. As he struck her, he felt his chest suffocating under waves of desperate sadness, like a child abandoned by its parents. That the evening's interrogation could have come to this... He had never in his wildest dreams imagined that it could have resulted in such a tragic scene. Yet he found soon enough that she was better prepared to face the situation than he. What would become of him after being jilted by this woman?... Not once had he entertained the thought.

'You can beat me all you like, but it won't change what you've already guessed. Yes, I'm in love with Serizawa! I've long been disgusted by you and your oafish ways.'

He had been expecting a revelation like this, but to hear it uttered with such piercing clarity made him unwittingly lower the hand in which he wielded the hanger. He was already long past the point of no return, however—and, realizing this, he was overcome by a feeling of unbearable loneliness.

'I'm sorry for what I've done. I'll say no more about it. Never shall I burden you again with my doubts, so, please, I beg of you, reconsider things and love me as you once did. Please, I'm begging you.'

He repeated these words over and again, kneeling before her, his head bowed in supplication. O-Tsuya's answer, however, was unwavering.

'There are matters that I, for my part, must also consider. Give me a few days to think it over.'

The killing of O-Tsuya took place two or three days after these events.

Fearing terribly that Shinsuke would resort to extreme measures, the young woman seemed to lose her customary audacity. She made her arrangements discreetly, and, when the time came, as the evening was already wearing on, she fled directly from the teahouse where she had been working. Shinsuke had been keeping watch for this for some time, and, as soon as he realized that she was intending to run away, he set out in pursuit, following her all the way to Mukōjima. In the end, just as they were passing the waterfront by torii of the Mimeguri shrine, O-Tsuya was dragged out of her palanquin by her arms and legs.

'Shinsuke, please, for the love of god!' she begged him while trying to hold back his arm. 'Let me see Serizawa just one last time before you take my life!'

Then, screaming for help, she turned around, attempting to flee under the blows of his sword. All the while, right until the very last, she kept crying out the name of her new lover, Serizawa.

THE SIREN'S
LAMENT

A LONG, LONG TIME AGO, when the House of Aisin-Gioro sat upon the dragon throne and the Qing dynasty still flourished with all the dazzling splendour of peonies in June, there lived in the capital of Nanjing a handsome young prince by the name of Meng Shidao. At a certain time, the father of this prince had served at the imperial court in Beijing, where his talents had won for him the favour of the Qianlong Emperor as well as the envy of his peers. His reward was a vast fortune that ostracized him from society, and later, when his only son was yet in his infancy, he quit this world entirely. A short while thereafter, the boy's mother followed in the footsteps of the father, and so the Prince, having been left an orphan, found himself quite naturally the sole heir to this veritable mountain of gold, silver and precious stones.

Since he was young, rich and had inherited, moreover, the prestige of a family of noble lineage, he had much already to be happy about. Yet fate had seen fit to grant the Prince even more, bestowing on him a countenance of rare beauty and a mind endowed with exceptional qualities.

Colossal wealth, elegant and refined features, an incisive wit: none of the youth in Nanjing could compete with him on any of these merits. Whether it was in offering sumptuous entertainments, in vying for the affections of a beautiful maiden from the Royal Academy, or in shining through the brilliance of his poetry, he put paid to every last one of them. What was more, all the women of the pleasure quarters in Nanjing dreamt of making the handsome Prince their lover, be it for a month or even a fortnight.

When at last he had his locks of adolescence cut, Shidao, abandoning himself to this way of life, began without delay to sample the wines of the pleasure quarters and, to use the parlance of those days, to acquire a taste for 'stealing the treasures of jade and incense'—so much so, in fact, that by the age of twenty-two or thereabouts he had tried every extreme that this world could offer by way of extravagance and debauchery. Perhaps it was for this reason that he had fallen lately into a kind of stupor and, no longer finding interest in any of the places he frequented, ended up cloistering himself away all day in his mansion, watching dreamily on as the days and months slipped by.

'What's the matter with you, Shidao? You've been remarkably out of sorts of late. Come, why don't we go and find ourselves some amusement in town? A man of your age isn't yet old enough to have grown weary of life's pleasures.'

Whenever these companions in debauchery would come and invite the Prince to join them, he would fix them in his languorous gaze and, with a smile of contempt, reply disdainfully:

'Hmm… As it just so happens, I haven't yet wearied of life's pleasures. But if I were to come with you, I wonder… Would there be anything to pique my interest? After all, I've exhausted all the women and the wines that this tired city has to offer. But if you have anything truly delicious for me, I am forever ready to accompany you…'

It was clear to see in the Prince's eyes, however, that he thought rather pitiful the life of his friends who, year after year, indulged in the same women from the same pleasure quarters and revelled in the tedium of debauchery. If he were to indulge in a woman, she had to be exceptional; if he were to revel in debauchery, it would always have to be something truly new. Even though such desires burned in the Prince's heart, he could not locate suitable objects with which to satisfy them, and so, finding himself in an impossible situation, he whiled away the hours in idleness.

And yet, although Shidao's fortune may have been inexhaustible, his life had its limits, and he could not expect to retain his youthful good looks for ever. Every now and then, this thought would give him a sudden yearning for pleasure, and the notion that he could no longer languish idly would assail him. One day he was struck by the desire to take this indolent existence of his in hand, before his youth had vanished entirely, and to steep his cooling heart in emotions as hot as boiling water. He longed to regain the feeling of excitement that he had enjoyed two or three years previously, when, immersed in merrymaking night after night and feasting day after day, he had not yet known the meaning of indifference. While such thoughts may have stirred him, though, they in no way offered radically new means by which he might now raise himself to the seventh heaven: after all, the terrestrial world could hardly contain yet more unusual pleasures for a man who had already pushed debauchery to its last limits and exhausted the well of extravagance.

And so, for want of anything better, the Prince had all the fine and rare wines without exception brought up from the cellars and served at his table. He then ordered that seven girls excelling in both wit and looks be chosen from among the beauties who had gathered from the four corners of the realm to crowd the capital's Royal Academy, and took them all as concubines, installing each of them in their own apartment. As for the drinks, he was first served a Luan-jiu, a sweet and potent wine from Shanxi, followed by a Huiquan-jiu, a light and mellow vintage from Changzhou; then came a Fuzhen-jiu from Suzhou and a Wuchengxun-jiu from Huzhou. There were famous rarities from each of the four hundred provinces—from the north, grape wine, fermented mare's milk and the liqueurs of pear and jujube; from the south, fermented coconut milk and distillations of tree sap and honey—and these heady wines and perfumed liqueurs followed one upon the other unceasingly in a variety of drinking vessels, moistening the young Prince's lips. But even these libations were powerless to bring new sensations to his palate, which had tasted of them many times before. Though the drinks intoxicated him, and though he found the intoxication pleasant, he was left, nonetheless, longing for something else, for the excitement of old that would send his spirit soaring up to the heavens—and that would well up in his breast no more.

Intrigued by this, the seven concubines wondered among themselves why their lord and master was sunk in such profound melancholy day after day, his face a picture of boredom, and so they called upon all the secrets of their art to lift the spirits of the young Prince. The first of them, Hong-Hong—so called 'the crimson beauty'—who prided herself on her playing, would take out her precious erhu whenever possible and sing with all the mellifluous intonations of her jade voice. The second, Ying-Ying—'the little nightingale'—knew how to turn a beautiful phrase, so that whenever the occasion called for it, she would pick up an interesting and amusing subject and, like a songbird, let her red tongue and golden beak warble freely upon this theme. The third concubine, Yao-Niang—'the modest maiden'—was famed for the whiteness and beauty of her skin, and, whenever the wine went to her head, she had a tendency to display with great pride her divinely smooth and fleshy arms. The fourth, Jin-Yun—'the cloud brocade'—counted on the charms of her coquetry, on the dimples that adorned her full cheeks, and on the radiant smile that revealed a row of teeth as regular as pomegranate seeds. As for the fifth, six and seventh concubines, they all did likewise, each offering her advantages, each vying for His Highness's favour. However, for all their maidenly charms, the Prince gave no sign of harbouring especial attachment to any of them. Certainly, by any worldly measure, these beauties were indeed peerless, but for the haughty young Prince it was much the same as the savour of the wines: their rare charms no longer held anything capable of surprising or seducing him. Thus, he sought unceasingly the next heady thrill that would plunge him body and soul into interminable pleasures and infinite ecstasies, but it was not within the power of women or ordinary wines to satisfy his desires.

'Since money is no object, is there really no rarer or more outlandish spirit that you have to offer? No woman of greater beauty?'

The merchants who called at the young Prince's palace were forever met with this request, but never yet had there been one with so exquisite an article that might win his approval. Rumour of his eccentricities had spread to the four corners of the empire, and so among them, attracted by the lure of lucre, were all manner of cheats and frauds who came from afar to palm off the most curious fakes.

'Sire, I have here a liqueur of a more than a thousand-year vintage, which I found in Xi'an, in the cellars of a wine merchant of the most well established and venerable repute. I am told that it is the famed Xuannao-jiu liqueur, made from the brains of the swallow, of which, in the days of the Tang dynasty, the Empress Zhang herself was so fond. I have also another Tang rarity: the Emperor Shunzong's favourite Longgao-jiu, a cordial distilled from the fat of the dragon. If there are doubts, may it please Your Highness to scrutinize the patina of the jug and see how the thousand-year-old seal has remained perfectly intact.'

Faced with this kind of proposition, the young Prince would listen first in a perverse silence before uttering some cutting remark.

'Please… Your eloquence is admirable, but if it is your intention to deceive me, you would do better to have a little more learning. That amphora was fired in the kilns of Nanjing, in the province of Jiangnan, and could have come only from the Southern Song dynasty. The very idea that the choicest wine of the Tang dynasty could be sealed in an amphora dating from the Song period is just too comical.'

At this, the merchant broke out in a cold sweat and, without so much as a word, took his leave.

In truth, such observations were not limited to porcelain, for whether it was clothing, precious stones, paintings or even arms, the connoisseurship of the young nobleman in every field of both fine and applied arts was so vast that it put the combined knowledge of scholars and antiquarians throughout the Celestial Empire to shame.

Those who came to trade in women flocked in numbers so great as to be a nuisance, and each sang the praises of his own merchandise with wild abandon.

'Sire, this time, I assure you, I've found you a jewel! She was born to a family of merchants in Hangzhou and is called Hualichun, "the beautiful flower of spring". Though she may be going on sixteen, her beauty should speak for itself, and she has mastered the arts and is skilled in poetry. Truly, Your Highness will not find another girl so accomplished in all the four hundred provinces. If you doubt my word, Sire, then may it please you to examine the goods for yourself.'

Although the young Prince had let himself be carried away time and again by such tall tales, in the end his heart would be stirred each time, and he would not be satisfied until he had examined the girl in question.

'Very well. I would meet her, so have her summoned forthwith'—such would be his reply in most instances.

However, when the traders brought their fine wares to the palace for an audience with the young Prince, unless they were of a wholly brazen nature, they would usually blush with shame and, in floods of tears, end up beating a hasty retreat. Indeed, the trader and the girl would first be ushered into a grand chamber of exceeding luxury, where they would be made to wait a long while, only after which would they be made to tread upon a floor of flower porphyry, which was as smooth as a mirror, along a corridor, which, after innumerable turns, finally led them to the interior apartments at the rear of the palace. There, before their very eyes, they would find a lavish banquet in full swing: leaning against pillars, musicians would be playing the bamboo flute; others, resting against a partition screen, would be playing the pipa; while a great crowd of men and women would be staggering about, mingling with one another, cup in hand, and, to the sound of Chinese gongs and drums, give themselves over to riotous dance and raucous song. This spectacle was, of itself, astounding enough; however, they would, moreover, find the host himself lying there on a carpet of flowers, sheltered under a canopy of the finest brocade, yawning extravagantly, indifferent to the hubbub going on all around him as he inhaled opium from a long silver pipe.

'Ah, yes. A beauty without peer in all the four hundred provinces, you say?…'

Sitting up slowly, the Prince would fix the visitors with a languid gaze. But before they had time to agree with him, he would laugh mockingly in their faces.

'Well, if that is so, then it would appear that the four hundred provinces are far poorer in women than I was led to believe. If you mean to go on in the business of selling flesh, then you would do well to take a good look at my own concubines for future reference.'

At the sound of their lord and master's voice, the seven concubines would appear immediately, streaming in from a chink in an embroidered curtain, one after another, just like tame doves. They had each freely chosen the sumptuous gauzes and silks that enswathed them, as well as the ornaments in their elaborate coiffures; each was accompanied by two handsome young attendants sporting double-topknots, who, as they followed them, wafted over the maidens' beautiful rose-hued cheeks a constant and gentle breeze from their long-handled fans stretched with finest gossamer. They lingered there by the Prince, exchanging silent glances all the while, like seven sovereigns with proud, radiant smiles upon their lips. The longer the silence continued, the more brilliantly their beauty shone—and no matter how consumed by greed were the traders, they could not but be enchanted by what they saw. Yet after a moment of transfixion punctuated by the batting of enraptured eyelashes, they finally recovered their wits, and, realizing the paltriness and ugliness of their own wares, they quickly took their leave and, scuttling off in embarrassment, fled the palace. As the young Prince followed their retreating shadows with his gaze, his face would be tinged with disappointment, and so, with a feeling of deep dejection, he would roll over and go back to sleep.

Soon enough, the summer of that year drew to a close, then autumn too grew old; the festivals of the tenth lunar month came and went, and the solemn birthday of the Great Sage was celebrated. Yet the languor and melancholy that haunted the young Prince's mind persisted, with no opportunity to dispel them. He would, moreover, turn twenty-five the following year—he who had relied so much on the freshness of his youth—and when he thought about it, he had the distinct impression that decrepitude was gradually consuming him, right down to the lustre of his luxuriant locks. As his dejection worsened and his desolation grew, so his thirst for pleasure increased and his impatience for the excitement that his heart demanded became even more acute. He took to drinking wine that was devoid of taste and would find himself in the arms of girls who were devoid of looks; he would carouse for two or three weeks at a time and carried on outrageously, trying a thousand and one things; yet none of this had the least effect on him. The result of it was that he would take to smoking opium again and, trying to devour his nightmares like the great chimera Mo, lose himself in clouds of grotesque delirium, spending his days in idleness, doing nothing but stretching his arms and legs.

The clouds that darkened the brow of the young Prince had not yet cleared when at last the New Year was ushered in and a new season of tranquillity began. In those days, the beneficence of the great Qing rulers shone newly over all the territories of the empire, and now that the peoples of the Eighteen Provinces were governed by an enlightened emperor, peace could be celebrated in joyous libations; and so, as the New Year was welcomed throughout Nanjing, there was a liveliness that had not been known in recent times. Now came the six days of the Festival of Lanterns, from the thirteenth day of the new moon, when the lanterns are put up, until they are taken down again on the eighteenth day, when night after night, at every gate of every house, hanging lanterns are lit, and the upper floors of official buildings and grand mansions are decked in draperies of silk crêpe and adorned with gaily coloured lights, and banquets are put on and music is played. Across the main thoroughfares in the heart of the city, lengths of cotton fabric had been slung from one side of the street to the other, from awning to awning, just as they do in Japan in the streets of Osaka at the height of summer, and they had built stands and mounts for lanterns of all kinds, auspicious red and white, which were hung on them. All throughout the streets, youths had gathered to form processions that moved to the noisy rhythms of gongs and cymbals as they carried lanterns of various effigies — dragon lanterns, horse lanterns, even lion lanterns—all of which called to mind the devotees of the Nichiren sect, who bear upon their shoulders some ten thousand lanterns during the celebrations given in honour of their founder. And yet, even at the height of these festivities, the face of the young Prince was still sunk in melancholy—one that no lantern could brighten.

It was early evening, two or three days after the festival began. The Prince had gone out onto the south-facing terrace, from which there was a magnificent view, and, as he reclined there on the daybed, he puffed away at the opium in his silver pipe. It so happened that his gaze fell directly on the street, where the thronging crowd was almost within reach: the hundreds and thousands of lanterns, all lit, at once swept past, ablaze in the argent mist of dusk, making the twilit cobblestones glint like fish-scales. At the crossroads of one of the main thoroughfares, a makeshift stage had been hastily improvised with banners waving in the wind, while two actors in garish costumes were putting on little pantomimes to the sound of accompanying music. In the eyes of the young Prince, who had not drawn a breath of fresh air in a long while, cloistered as he was in the recesses of his palace, this sudden spectacle aroused in him a curious sensation, as though he had found himself in the capital of a faraway exotic land—unless, of course, he was simply in the grip of some extraordinary hallucination brought on by the opium. Before he knew it, he had abandoned his pipe, and was leaning over the balustrade of the terrace, his chin resting on his hands as he gazed out vacantly at the frenetic bustle of the street. Just then, in small groups of threes and fives, a procession of people in masks began to line up, and, as though to assuage the Prince's melancholy, they set off with remarkable speed, stamping in time with one another and letting out cries of joyous celebration. After them came a troupe of carriers holding aloft lanterns whose shapes evoked all manner of birds and fish.

It was then that the young Prince's gaze fell on a strange figure, whom he began to follow with rapt attention for quite some while. The man in question had on a velvet hat, a scarlet woollen cape and jet-black leather shoes; he was leading along a donkey that was pulling a carriage of some kind. Each element of his outfit, from the shoes to the hat, was covered in holes and patches where the colour had faded—the vestiges, no doubt, of a long journey. Just in front of him was an imposing dragon-lantern illuminated by countless candles, one of the most spectacular dimensions, which must easily have been the height of three or even four men and whose dozens of bearers chanted as they advanced along their route. The man did not seem to have any connection with the troupe, however, and whenever he stopped, which he would do from time to time, he would let out a sigh of genuine exhaustion as he followed the commotion in the street. He might have been taken for an isolated member of one or other of the troupes in the parade, but as he gradually made his way to the palace of the young Prince, this initial impression was belied by the way in which he led the donkey and the carriage. In fact, everything about him indicated a foreigner: his clothes, of course, but also his complexion, his hair, even the colour of his eyes.

He must be a man of the Western race. One of those Dutchmen, perhaps, who has reached our shores from the islands in the South Seas... Thus ran the young Prince's thoughts. This was, of course, a time when Europeans were occasionally seen in the streets of Nanjing, but how could the Prince fail to be intrigued by this man and his extraordinary ways, not least when, dragging his weary legs, he roamed about while the festivities were in full swing, like a beggar buffeted by the surging waves of revellers in the procession. Stranger still was that the man, having reached the spot just below the terrace of the palace, stopped abruptly and doffed his velvet hat, greeting the young Prince on the balcony with all due deference. Then, while motioning to the carriage to which his donkey was hitched, he began speaking with great urgency.

'I have in this carriage a remarkable creature that dwells at the bottom of the South Seas. Having heard tell of you, I have come from the shores of the distant tropics to show you this mermaid that I have captured alive.'

In the street, the noise of the festivities was so fierce that it was nigh impossible to hear him, but this was the general sense of what he had imparted in his faltering Chinese.

When the Prince heard on the lips of this Westerner the word 'mermaid' spoken in a strange accent to which his ear was unaccustomed, his heart immediately began to pound. Of course, never in his life had he set eyes on one of these creatures, but just now, hearing the word pronounced so unexpectedly by this traveller from the South Seas, with his exotic intonations, it was tinged with an even deeper mystery for him.

'Hullo! Hullo! Won't somebody go and fetch for me that red-headed man standing there forthwith!' said the Prince with exceeding haste to one of the servant girls waiting upon him.

Soon enough, the donkey was led into the inner sanctuary of the palace, passing through the great entrance gate, an interior door, and then another leading into a garden, which was laid out at the rear of the building, before being settled by the steps to a series of inner chambers that were illuminated as though it were daylight by the light of the red lanterns. Escorted as always by his seven concubines, the Prince made his way towards the end of the corridor, where a seat was offered him. Seeing this, the foreigner bowed once again with deep respect, and, after performing the ritual salutations required by etiquette, he resumed the tale with his outlandish pronunciation and faltering tongue.

'It was a few hundred leagues from the port of Canton, off the coast of one of the coral islands in the Dutch possessions, that I was able to get my hands on this mermaid. One day, while I was out fishing for pearls, quite by chance I happened to catch something far more precious and more beautiful. Man, of course, cannot love a pearl; but no man who sets eyes on a mermaid can help falling in love with her. The pearl offers only an icy brilliance, but, beneath her bewitching allure, the mermaid harbours hot tears, a warm heart, and a mysterious wisdom. The tears of the mermaid are a dozen times purer than the colour of the pearl. Her heart is a hundred times more scarlet than the most precious coral. And her wisdom opens up paths even more mysterious than those opened by the fakirs of India. And yet, although she possesses occult powers that are beyond the ken of man, she has been reduced to the ranks of a fish, lower even than the human race, because of her depravity. And so, while swimming in the deep blue of the azure seas, she longs for the paradise of dry land and, pining for the world of men, intones a lament that knows no rest. The proof is found in that any man can recognize the dolorous shadow of melancholy that veils the siren's beautiful face...'

As he spoke these words, the expression on the foreigner's face also saddened, as though sympathizing with the fate of the captive mermaid.

Even before the young Prince had been allowed to view the mermaid, he was deeply impressed by the foreigner's appearance. Until then, he had always believed these creatures known as Westerners to be semi-civilized savages, but the more he scrutinized the face of this beggar-cum-barbarian, the more he discovered in it a nobility and an authority that somehow managed to overwhelm him. The foreigner's green eyes, just like tropical seas of emerald and sapphire, beckoned his soul to fathomless depths. Moreover, with his well-defined eyebrows, his broad forehead, and his snow-white complexion, his face was incomparably more refined and handsome than that of the young Prince, who prided himself on his own beauty, not to mention capable of a richness of expression that showed every nuance of the most complex emotions.

The Prince had followed the tale of the mermaid that the foreigner related to him with rapture, and now, after a brief pause, he asked him:

'But tell me, from whom did you hear about me, to make so long a journey all the way to Nanjing?'

'It came about only recently, as it happens. I heard about you just the other day, in Macao, thanks to a merchant whom I chanced to meet in the street. Had I known about you before, I dare say you would have had the opportunity to see my mermaid well before now. I have had this extraordinary merchandise for some six months already, and since then I have toured all the lands of Asia, calling at every port worthy of the name, but no matter where I went, nobody—neither man of commerce, nor nobleman—was willing to acquire her. Some men demurred, claiming that the price was too high. Why, this mermaid is worth seventy diamonds of Arabia, eighty rubies of Cochinchina, as well as ninety peacocks from Annam and a hundred tusks of elephant ivory from Siam, and there can be no question of my letting her go for less than that. Others fled, dreading the mermaid's affections and trembling with fear. Why, since ancient times, no man loved by a mermaid has been able to spare himself, for, before he knows it, he will fall into the trap set by her uncanny charms and, after being depleted body and soul, he will disappear like a ghost from our world without anyone knowing whither he has vanished. That is why whosoever values his fortune or his life cannot acquire with impunity what I have to sell. Although I have laid my hands on an extraordinary rarity, I have pursued these fruitless wanderings for such a very long time, wasting my days without anyone to take me seriously. Perhaps if I hadn't heard about you from this merchant in Macao, I might have found myself burdened with this precious cargo for a good while yet. From what the merchant told me, this young Prince from Nanjing was the only man who would acquire my mermaid, for he was ready, he said, to give his life and his immense fortune in the pursuit of pleasure and lamented that there was nothing worthy of this gesture. He said that, having already exhausted the delicacies and delights of all the earth, this young Prince was in search of a phantom beauty that was not of this world. He was the one, he said, who was certain to buy my mermaid.'

Would the Prince buy his merchandise or not? The foreigner did not seem to doubt the outcome of the deal in the slightest. He had offered the Prince these terms, as though he had read his heart. What was more, the foreigner's attitude, far from provoking hostility in the Prince, had instead raised him to an irrepressible point of exaltation. As the Prince heard out the foreigner's explanations, he had the distinct impression that he was receiving an imperative command to buy the mermaid, an impression that this acquisition had been an act inscribed in his destiny long ago.

'What this merchant has told you is indeed the truth. I am the one described to you by that man in Macao. Just as you have been searching for me, I, too, have been searching for you. And just as you trust in me, I, too, shall trust in you. I shall buy your mermaid this very minute, and at the price you have just named, without even taking the precaution of inspecting the merchandise first.'

Rising up from the depths of his heart, these words passed his lips before even he was truly conscious of them. And so, the promised diamonds, rubies, peacocks and elephant tusks were immediately taken from the coffers of the five warehouses and the aviaries in his parkland and brought to the terrace, where they were piled up high in front of the stone steps. The foreigner, however, did not show the least astonishment at this demonstration of the Prince's great fortune; instead, after having counted the goods calmly and methodically, he went over and lifted the curtain of the carriage, thus revealing the body of a captive mermaid consumed by sadness.

She was enclosed in a beautiful glass aquarium, the lower half of her body covered in scales and coiled up like a serpent, pressing against the glass wall. Suddenly, as though seized by shame at being exposed to the glaring light of the world of men, she folded her head down upon her breast and, with her hands clasped at the small of her back, just sat there, a picture of sorrow. Her height was about that of any human, so the vessel into which her entire body fitted must have been some six feet tall.

The interior was filled to the brim with seawater that was as translucent and as pure as gemstones, and, with each of the mermaid's sighs, she exhaled an infinite string of bubbles, which, like crystalline pearls, rose up to burst on the water's surface. After four or five servants had lifted the aquarium from the carriage and placed it on the floor of the chamber overlooking the palace garden, the light from the dozens of lanterns illuminating the room was immediately reflected on the naked body of the mermaid, and her skin, so fresh and smooth, began to glitter with an even more brilliant lustre, like a blazing fire.

'I had, until now, secretly prided myself on my vast knowledge and expertise. There was nothing that had ever existed upon this earth at one time or another, from the most precious creature to the rarest treasure, about which I knew not everything. However, even in my dreams, never had I imagined that such a beautiful creature could dwell at the bottom of the sea. Nor, in all the world of fantasy that the opium conjures before my eyes, can any creature compete in grace and beauty with this siren. Even had she cost twice as much, I should not have hesitated to buy her from you...'

For all the Prince's eloquence, his words were insufficient to give full expression to the unceasing sense of amazement and admiration that was now flooding his heart. Why, no sooner had he witnessed the icy allure and melancholy pathos of the marine enchantress that had been set before him, than he felt in his soul a panicked trembling of indescribable force and violence, as if all the nerves in his body had instantly frozen. He stood there, transfixed, motionless, petrified like a corpse, his eyes trained on the splendid radiance of the light in the aquarium, while, mystifyingly, tears of deep emotion began surreptitiously to fall from his eyes. For several moments, he remained in thrall to this emotion for which he had so longed. At last, that supreme feeling of ecstasy had returned to him. Only yesterday had he hopelessly lamented the tedium of the long days and months—yet now that man was no more. He found himself once again in a state of mind that allowed him to go tearing along life's path under the constant spur of a profusion of thrills.

'I had always believed that the happiest fate upon this earth was to be born in human form. But if in the depths of the oceans there is a mysterious world where creatures as exquisite as this reside, then I would rather be lowered to the rank of sirens than remain a man. Enswathing my loins in a sumptuous robe of scales, I could then enjoy eternal love with this water nymph… Before the freshness of her eyes, the luxuriance of her black hair, the snowy whiteness of her skin, even the seven concubines waiting upon me seem ugly and vulgar by comparison. How common and quaint they now appear…'

As he spoke, the mermaid, having some unknown thought, slowly rippled her fins and, lifting her face, which she had kept lowered, gazed intently at the Prince.

The young Prince's knowledge was not limited to works of art—antiques, paintings and calligraphy—for he had also mastered the art of physiognomy that has been handed down in China since antiquity. However, in examining the mermaid's features to decipher the structure of her face, he discovered such odd particularities that were unable to be explained by the wisdom of this science. Certainly, she was the very image of a mermaid as they had been depicted in paintings, and there was no doubt that the lower part of her body was that of a fish, while the upper part was that of a human being. Yet as the Prince looked at different aspects of that upper body in isolation—the bone structure, the musculature, the facial features—he could see that they deviated markedly from their usual human counterparts. The features of the mermaid differed so much from those of any ordinary woman that the knowledge of physiognomy that the Prince had acquired could scarcely be applied. For instance, neither the shape nor the colour of her most hauntingly beautiful eyes conformed to any of the categories that he had studied. Her enormous eyes glittered a phosphorescent blue under the translucent water that filled the glass vessel. Sometimes the eyes would clear into an indigo so limpid that they might have been taken for pieces of crystal, two drops of water that had solidified in the water's midst, and in their depths there was a gentle grace, a sublime light lurking in the infinite abyss of her soul, which seemed to contemplate eternity. The shadowy halo of a faraway darkness shrouded in quiet beauty also hovered there, and there glinted a heavenly reflection of such resplendence and pathos that was beyond the spectrum of any human eye. The shape of her nose and eyebrows, too, gave the impression of an even more extraordinary design, an even more exalted beauty. Their appearance corresponded little to that so prized by Chinese physiognomy, with its eyebrows of 'new moon' or of 'willow leaf', and with its noses of 'sleeping rhinoceros' or of 'Tartar sheep'. For in the mermaid's features there dwelt a beauty closer to the gods than to men, a beauty that transcended conventional beauty, that went beyond the traditional harmony of mere mortals so as to attain immortal perfection. And when, with a movement full of languor, she moved her long neck, her dark emerald hair spread out, undulating like seaweed, quivering under the gentle ripples, sometimes falling on her forehead like a tangle of clouds and mist, or else rising and fanning out like the tail of a splendid peacock. This perfection was not merely limited to her face: it could be found in every part of her body that corresponded to that of a human. The line descending from the neck to the shoulder, and from the shoulder to the breast, traced an elegant curve, while the suppleness of her arms revealed a flawless symmetry; and whenever the muscles beneath her opulent flesh tensed and relaxed like a bow being drawn, her body exuded a strange and unfathomable harmony, one that combined the agility of a fish, the strength of a beast, the allure of a goddess, and was every bit as bewitching as all the colours of the rainbow combined. But what particularly caught the Prince's eye and melted his heart was in fact the snow-white unblemished immaculacy of her skin. Her skin was of such brilliant, luminous purity that the word 'white' scarcely did it justice; in fact, it was so white that it would have been more fitting to speak of its radiant lustre, for the skin covering her entire body glittered like the pupil of an eye. Indeed, the whiteness was such that made the Prince wonder whether there was not some luminous source concealed within her bones, radiating through her flesh with the intense brightness of the moon. And when the Prince approached and looked carefully, he noticed, on the surface of this miraculous skin, an infinity of white down, fine hairs that sprouted brilliantly and in little curls, with tiny bubbles at each of their ends, like roe, practically invisible to the naked eye—a patina of silver pearls that, like a silk gauze studded with precious gems, covered her whole body.

'Noble Prince! You have recognized the value of my mermaid far beyond what I anticipated. Through you, I have received sufficient reward and, at the same time, been able to lay my hands on a colossal fortune. In exchange for the mermaid that I have given you, I have loaded my carriage with these treasures of the Orient and shall now return to the port of Canton. From there, I shall then take the steamer and return to my native land, in the Far West, for there, in my country, there are many people who will prize these treasures just as you prize this mermaid… But before I go, it is my parting wish that you permit me to give the mermaid a farewell kiss.'

The foreigner then leant over the edge of the aquarium, while the mermaid, as fluid as quicksilver dancing in the waters, brought the upper half of her body to the surface and, enfolding both arms around the man's neck, remained thus for some while, cheek to cheek, shedding bitter tears. Pearling at the tips of her eyelashes, they rolled down to her chin, and, as the tears followed one upon another, a fragrant aroma with the scent of musk spread throughout the four corners of the room.

'Will you really not feel the mermaid's loss?' the young Prince asked. 'Can you really not regret having sold her to me for such a paltry sum? How is it that the people of your country prize those precious stones more than a mermaid?! Why did you elect not to take her back with you?'

The young Prince spoke in a sardonic tone, as if to mock the merchant's base nature, which had, for the sake of material gain, sacrificed a treasure of such beauty without the least remorse.

'Yes, it is altogether quite understandable that you should wonder these things. But, you see, mermaids are not so rare in the Occident. I hail from northern Europe, from a country called Holland. My home is on the banks of the Rhine, and in my childhood I learnt that mermaids have always inhabited the upper reaches of this river. Some have legs like a human, while others might be endowed with legs like those of birds. All the way from the depths of the Mediterranean to the wooded mountains and the stretches of water on the continent, they appear from time to time to seduce men. The poets and artists of my country have never ceased to sing their mysteries and paint their figures, and we have learnt all the many charms of the mermaid's beguiling smile and all the many dangers of her allure. Because of this, many European women, without going so far as to become sirens themselves, have devoted themselves to studying the mermaid's looks, and have each mastered something of their blue eyes, their white skin, and their well-proportioned limbs. If Your Highness finds it hard to believe me, may it please you to look at the features of my own face and the colour of my skin. Any native of the Occident, even one as unworthy as I, will inevitably possesses somewhere within him a nobility and an elegance of the same order as those of the mermaid.'

The Prince was unable to refute these words, for he had long since noticed the resemblance that there was, as the foreigner had just remarked, between the features of his face and those of the mermaid. Certainly, the degree of the Prince's admiration differed, but just as he was under the mermaid's spell, so too did he find himself in no small measure attracted to the foreigner's face. Although the man did not attain the perfection or delicate beauty of the mermaid, still he had the latent possibilities of attaining them some day. And, compared to the inhabitants of the territories of China, with their sallow skin and flat faces, he gave the impression of being altogether a creature of a race closer to that of the siren.

While Westerners roamed the oceans of the world in their little ships, the peoples of the East had remained convinced until then that the extent of the earth was, like

that of time, something without limit, and considered that
a terrestrial peregrination of a thousand or two thousand
leagues was an undertaking almost as difficult as living a
period of a hundred or two hundred years. So the young
Prince, educated though he had been in a great Asian
country, had never dreamt, despite his thirst for knowledge,
of crossing the seas to go there, under far-flung western
skies, to see this Europe that he imagined to be a barbarous
land inhabited by serpents and demons. But now that he
had, for the first time in his life, seen a Westerner with his
own eyes, now that he had heard him tell of his native
land, he could remain indifferent no longer.

'I had no idea that the Occident was such a beautiful and
noble place! If all the men of your country have as august
a face as yours, and if all the women of your country have
as white a skin as that of the mermaid, what an unspoilt
land, what a fair paradise Europe must be! Please, take the
mermaid and me back to your country and introduce us
among the superior race that resides there. There is nothing
to keep me in China any longer. Rather than remain a
prince and end my days in Nanjing, I should prefer to die
a lowly pauper in your country! Please, heed my request
and let me accompany you on the voyage!'

Brimming with enthusiasm, the young Prince threw
himself at the feet of the man and, grabbing at the hem of

his cloak, frantically pleaded his case. With an unnerving smile, the foreigner cut him off.

'I won't hear of it! It is my wish that, for your own sake, you stay here in Nanjing, loving this poor mermaid as deeply and for as long as you are able. Besides, I very much doubt that the inhabitants of Europe, however fair their complexion or beautiful their faces, would be able to satisfy you more than the mermaid you have in this aquarium. For it is in her that all the beauty and the sublime of the European ideal are embodied. You can find here, in the magnificent, voluptuous figure of this creature, the very quintessence of Western painting and poetry. And it is none other than this siren who, with her Western charms, will be able to delight your senses and bewitch your soul, revealing to you the apogee of beauty. Even if you were to visit her homeland, you would surely find nothing to surpass this splendour...'

Then some thought must have crossed the foreigner's mind, for a look of sorrow clouded his brow and the tone of his voice darkened. Suddenly, he changed the subject.

'Either way, I pray most sincerely for your happiness and longevity. I can tell that you are already in love with her, so I pray also that you shall be able to overturn the legend in my country which holds that calamity soon befalls anyone who seeks the love of a mermaid. I should not think of asking for your precious life in return for her. If, by chance, I should come back some day to visit the Asian continent, and if fortune so wills it that I should meet Your Highness again, then on that occasion, I shall take you with me. But as for that… ah, as for that… I foresee nothing but sorrows.'

No sooner had these words been spoken than the foreigner bowed deeply once again and, leading away the donkey, which pulled behind it a carriage groaning under the mountain of treasure obtained in exchange for the mermaid, melted into the darkness of the palace garden.

Ever since the mermaid's acquisition, the residence of the young Prince had been plunged into silence. The seven concubines were confined to their apartments, no longer summoned by their lord and master. The echoes of joyous celebrations, of the dances and songs that night after night had animated every part of the palace, had fallen mute, and all those who were in service there had been reduced to sighing.

'There was something queer about that foreign devil!' the servants would say. 'Coming here and selling snake oil like that. Let's hope that things don't get any worse…'

Such remarks were exchanged in whispers, accompanied by significant looks. Not a single one of them

JUN'ICHIRŌ TANIZAKI

had been given the opportunity to lift the curtain in the chamber where the aquarium had been placed, and not one of them had been allowed to approach the mermaid. Only the young Prince, the master of the household, was permitted to do so. Separated by a simple wall of glass, he and the mermaid would face each other in silence all day long, she breathing heavily underwater and he tormenting himself outside, one lamenting the fate that forbade her to leave her watery element, while the other cursed his inability to dive right into it. And so, the gloomy and desolate hours passed by. Sometimes the Prince would circle around the glass walls, looking morose, begging her to emerge from the waters and offer him a glimpse of even part of her naked body. But as soon as he made to approach, the mermaid's shoulders would stiffen, and she would shrink even more, as though frightened by something, and cower at the bottom of the water. Once night fell, the tears that rolled from her eyes gave off, just as the foreigner said they would, a pearlescent light that glowed like brilliant fireflies amid the darkness of the room. Her bluish-white tears beaded drop by drop, and when they began to float in the water, then the ill-fated beauty of her body, the nobility as serene as that of the moon goddess Chang'e in her firmament of celestial bodies, would come to prick and haunt the heart of the young man, like a ghost emerging from the nocturnal darkness into the light of the will-o'-the-wisps.

It so happened that one evening the Prince, overwhelmed with pain and sorrow, had filled his carved jade cup with a precious Shaoxing wine and was enjoying the sensation of the fiery, potent liquor spreading through his body and warming his belly, when the mermaid, who had by then shrivelled away to the size of a sea cucumber, suddenly rose to the surface with a supple movement, attracted perhaps by the perfume of the hot wine, and reached her arms out of the aquarium. Scarcely had the Prince brought to her lips the cup that he held in his hands, when, losing all restraint, she impulsively stuck out a scarlet tongue and, applying the sea sponge that was her lips to the rim of the cup, drank it dry in a single gulp. Then, with a lurid smile, like that of Beardsley's Salome in *The Dancer's Reward*, she insistently demanded another cup, purring all the while.

'If you like wine so much, I'll give you as much to drink as you please. Were an ardent intoxication to warm your veins that are being dulled by the cold water of the seas, you would surely become only more beautiful! Then, perhaps you would be able to show more affection, more warmth, more humanity, too. If I am to believe the Dutchman who came to sell you, you are, it would seem, possessed of such occult powers that man cannot fathom. You are also possessed, I am told, of a lustful and corrupt nature. I should very much like you to show me these occult powers. I should like to touch this lust with my own hands! If you truly can exercise this strange magic, then tonight, for this one night, take on human form for me. And if you really are of unbridled lust, then stop crying like that and respond to my love.'

But when, having spoken these words, the young Prince tried to offer her his lips instead of the cup, the inscrutable mermaid's face suddenly clouded over, like a mirror misted by breath.

'Oh, Prince! Forgive me, please. Have some pity and forgive me!' she suddenly said in plain human speech. 'Thanks to the power of this cup of wine that you have had the graciousness to offer me, I have at last recovered the strength to speak in the language of men... As the Dutchman told you, my home is in Europe, in the Mediterranean Sea. If ever you happen to visit the West someday, you must visit a southern land called Italy, for it is truly the most beautiful country of all, where each landscape is a veritable painting. Once your boat, after passing the Strait of Messina, brings you off the port of Naples, you will find yourself near a place where a group

of mermaids has lived since antiquity. It is said that in
the past, when the enchantingly melodious song of the
siren echoed from who could say where, the sailors who
navigated those coastal waters were seduced and, before
they knew it, lured down into the depths of the abyss…
But last year, towards the end of April, even though I was
living in that beloved spot, I carelessly let myself be carried
by the warm spring currents, and, lost, I ended up drifting
as far as the archipelagos of the South Seas. Then, one
day, while I was resting my fins on a beach, in the shade
of a palm tree, I experienced the humiliation of falling
captive to man and seeing my body exposed shamelessly
in all the marketplaces of least renown in Asia. Oh, noble
Prince! Have pity on me and release me without delay into
the vast expanse of the sea. Whatever magical powers I
possess, I can do nothing with them so long as I remain
captive in this narrow vessel. Here, my life and my beauty
do nothing but fade away. If you really desire to see the
magic of the mermaid, then please, return me to the
homeland I so long for.'

'If you pine for the sea of southern Europe so very
much, it must surely be because you have a lover there.
Somewhere in the depths of the Mediterranean, there
must be a handsome man with the body of a fish, too, who
waits there, yearning for you night and day. Otherwise,

JUN'ICHIRŌ TANIZAKI

you would not despise me so. Why else would you so cruelly spurn my love and wish to return to your native waters?'

As the young Prince gave voice to his resentment, the mermaid, her head bowed and eyes closed, listened, at first humbly, but then, with a graceful movement of her arms, she gripped the Prince by the shoulders: 'Ah, but why ever should I despise a handsome young man like you, and of such rare nobility? Why ever should I be so bereft of feeling that I could remain indifferent to you? If you want proof of my love, then just listen to the beating of my heart!'

With a brisk movement, the mermaid fanned her tail fin, and no sooner had she pressed her back to the edge of the aquarium than she then arched her body like a bow, her head thrown back in a splash of droplets, her hair trailing to the ground. Then, like a monkey hanging from a branch, she reached out her arms and wrapped them around the young Prince. He felt a strange, cold sensation about his neck, where his skin came into contact with the mermaid's, as though a block of ice had been applied to it, and, before he knew it, his neck had frozen. The more the mermaid tightened her embrace, the more the icy cold that emanated from her snow-white skin penetrated his bones, piercing him to the marrow—and so his body, warmed by the intoxication of the Shaoxing wine, suddenly grew numb. Just as the Prince could endure the deathly cold no longer, the mermaid took hold of his wrists and placed them to her heart.

'Although my body has the coldness of a fish, my heart has the warmth of a human. Here is the proof of my love for you.'

At these words, the young Prince felt a warmth enter his palms, like a blazing fire within a ball of snow. Beneath his fingers that caressed the mermaid's left breast, he felt, just below the ribs, the vigorous rhythm of a beating heart; then, in every vein throughout his body, his blood began to circulate once again, beating with life.

'For all the heat of my blood and all the intensity of my feelings,' the mermaid continued, 'my skin yet quivers unceasingly from this wretched cold. Even on the rare occasion that I set eyes on an attractive man, the mermaid's miserable lot that my karma has earnt me prevents me from ever loving him. The curse of the gods has reduced me to the rank of a fish living underwater, which is why, whatever the passion that I may feel for a man, I can only ever suffer a thousand torments, a slave to my unbridled fantasies, driven mad by the flames of lust. Oh, Prince! Let me return to my marine abode, deliver me from this shame and this distress. Hidden away beneath the cold blue waves, I shall surely manage to forget the rigours of my pitiful lot. If you deign to lend a sympathetic ear to my plight, then I shall reward you with a demonstration of my magical powers.'

'Oh, yes! Show me your magic! In exchange, I shall grant all the wishes that you care to name.'

Once the Prince had let slip these rash words, the mermaid clapped her hands together with joy and prostrated herself several times in a sign of profound gratitude.

'Oh, Prince! I shall bid you farewell, then. Once I have metamorphosed with the help of my magic, you will surely regret your words. But if you wish to see me again as a mermaid, you must embark on a steamer bound for Europe, and, as it crosses the Equator, you must go up on deck one fine moonlit evening and cast me back into the sea unseen. I promise you that, having become a mermaid once again, I shall emerge from the waves and give you due thanks.'

No sooner was it said than done. Taking on the pallor of a jellyfish, the mermaid's body vanished like a block of melting ice, leaving behind in the aquarium a small sea snake some two or three feet in length, bobbing up and down, the blues and greens of its back glinting in the water.

*

It was in the early spring of that same year when, following the instructions given by the mermaid, the young Prince embarked from Hong Kong on board a steamer bound for England. Then, one evening, after a stopover in Singapore, the Prince climbed up onto a deserted deck bathed in moonlight just as the ship was crossing the Equator. He approached the gunwale and, discreetly taking out a glass jar that he had been holding tightly to his chest, released the small sea snake that was imprisoned there. As though regretting this separation, the creature wrapped itself two or three times around the Prince's wrist, then, having left his fingers a few moments later, moved off, gliding smoothly across the surface of a sea as slick as oil. And so, cutting through the golden rippling of the waves on which the moonbeams broke, she continued to meander, her fine scales shimmering all the while, before finally disappearing into the water.

Five or six minutes passed. Far off, towards the infinity of the open sea, where the most intense light dazzled the surface of the waters, a fearless creature leapt up like a flying fish, raising a great spray of silvery foam. When the Prince turned in this direction, amazed by the bewitching figure that shone so brightly that one could easily have taken it for the lunar hare having fallen from the sky into the sea, the siren, already half buried under the spray, raised aloft both her arms and let out a long and plaintive cry, before plunging into a whirlpool and sinking beneath the waves.

Carrying as its cargo the last glimmer of hope that yet remained in the Prince's heart, the ship continued on its way to the Europe of his cherished dreams, gradually drawing nearer to the native Mediterranean of the siren.

STEFAN ZWEIG · EDGAR ALLAN POE · ISAAC BABEL
TOMÁS GONZÁLEZ · ULRICH PLENZDORF · JOSEPH KESSEL
VELIBOR ČOLIĆ · LOUISE DE VILMORIN · MARCEL AYMÉ
ALEXANDER PUSHKIN · MAXIM BILLER · JULIEN GRACQ
BROTHERS GRIMM · HUGO VON HOFMANNSTHAL
GEORGE SAND · PHILIPPE BEAUSSANT · IVÁN REPILA
E.T.A. HOFFMANN · ALEXANDER LERNET-HOLENIA
YASUSHI INOUE · HENRY JAMES · FRIEDRICH TORBERG
ARTHUR SCHNITZLER · ANTOINE DE SAINT-EXUPÉRY
MACHI TAWARA · GAITO GAZDANOV · HERMANN HESSE
LOUIS COUPERUS · JAN JACOB SLAUERHOFF
PAUL MORAND · MARK TWAIN · PAUL FOURNEL
ANTAL SZERB · JONA OBERSKI · MEDARDO FRAILE
HÉCTOR ABAD · PETER HANDKE · ERNST WEISS
PENELOPE DELTA · RAYMOND RADIGUET · PETR KRÁL
ITALO SVEVO · RÉGIS DEBRAY · BRUNO SCHULZ · TEFFI
EGON HOSTOVSKÝ · JOHANNES URZIDIL · JÓZEF WITTLIN